DARKENED SHADOWS: THE REVENGE

A. WATKINS

This is a work of fiction. Names, characters, places, and incidents are products of the author's imagination or are used fictitiously and are not to be construed as real. Any resemblance to actual events, locations, organizations, or persons, living or dead, is entirely coincidental.

World Castle Publishing, LLC
Pensacola, Florida
Copyright © A. Watkins 2016
Paperback ISBN: 9781955086028
eBook ISBN: 9781629894195
First Edition World Castle Publishing, LLC, January 18, 2016
http://www.worldcastlepublishing.com
Cover: Karen Fuller
Editor: Maxine Bringenberg

CHAPTER 1

Emily

She paced around the small living room of the apartment as she thought. A year had passed, and still, she was surrounded by imbeciles. The only information she had accumulated was what Abraham had told her. Collin had never given her the information she needed. They had both known that the siblings would be of great use in taking over the human world, yet he'd told her nothing before he was defeated. When that damn little girl Cameron had defeated him.

"Now, remind me again, who is Zalvana Peythron?" Emily called.

"Zalvana Peythron, one of light, ancestor of my wife, and children...powerful."

"Why was she supposedly with my father?"

"Unknown...journal...."

"What journal?"

She looked over at Jack, Cameron and Abraham's biological father, who was leaning back on the couch before her with blank eyes. His hair was matted, and his face had grown a rather messy beard. Emily paced once more, processing the information in her mind. Abraham had spoken of Zalvana Peythron, a name that Collin had also mentioned. If she were going to defeat the Evans siblings, she would need to find out how to destroy their whole line. Her brother would be brought back to her...the only family she had, even if he was an idiot and impatient.

She sat on the couch next to Jack, whose limp body fell over slightly. "Cameron and Abraham are of something else. Only Collin knew what, so here I am, sitting alone. I must investigate further and deeper. I must find this journal." She glanced over at Jack. "Thank you for inviting me over, traitor. Now forget we ever spoke." Jack's eyes turned over and then returned to their natural color. Emily snapped her fingers and, in an instant, was at the doorway of Abraham's home.

"Abraham, dear, I'm back!" she called, hurrying up the stairs to their bedroom. Upon reaching it, she found Abraham standing in front of the farthest window, clipping on a tie to his tux. His hair was brushed back, showing his forehead. "Why, don't you look dashing?" She snarled to him as she hurried over to the closet to fetch her dress. "Must we go?" she pleaded, turning to him. He looked at her then.

"You don't have to if you don't want to, sweetheart," he said.

She sneered at his response. "I won't have you going alone."

Abraham went to her, took the dress from her, and laid it on the bed next to them. Taking her hands into his, he said, "I wouldn't want to go alone." Then he kissed her deeply.

Cameron

After applying the glossy lip balm, I looked at my reflection in the mirror. My hair had grown a couple of inches and was nearly at the base of my waist, and with my body having gone through the change, I looked like a completely different person than I had just a year ago. My face was much clearer—acne was no longer a problem—I had lost the black circles that once existed under my eyes, and even the freckles that were once on my nose had disappeared. As a human, my eyes had been hazel. But after the change, they changed to a much brighter green…unlike the Virgos, whose eyes were a tiny bit darker than mine because of their Were gene. Nonetheless, I couldn't complain. Maybe I should just be thankful I didn't look old. Abraham sure hadn't changed, from the moment he went missing till he was brought back. While under Collin's control, Abraham was dirty, with pale skin and red eyes. Thankfully, he looked much better now, with some color in his cheeks and natural blue eyes. Gathiens were pale, and each had their own shade of red eyes, between bright blood red to dark, dry red. Abraham's looks changed because Collin dropped his control over him when I killed Collin, making him look much more human. But that wasn't the case, because Abraham and I weren't human at all…actually, we didn't have any idea what we were. Obviously, we were not Were because we couldn't change into a werewolf, and obviously, we had some kind of Gathien gene in our system, but wouldn't that mean there was something else inside of us? What was this other half? Perhaps we just didn't age because of that secret part inside of us, and that honestly scared me.

Why would someone want to live forever? I'd seen movies and read books about vampires who, as the undead, lived forever. We were different from vampires in many ways, but what if we didn't age…like them? I felt like being a vampire would have been sad and lonely, living forever and knowing the people you loved would move on without you. I, for one, couldn't do it. I hoped that sooner rather than later, I would find out more about my and Abraham's family history.

It had been a year and one month since Collin was defeated. During the time Abraham was in Collin's control, he never received any kind of information about our family until the day Collin died. We found out about Zalvana Peythron, sure, but that name only led us to a dead end. Jack said he was clueless about the name, and even looking up her name in the database gave us nothing. But for now, that wasn't something to worry about. Abraham was back and well, and everything was almost back to normal. Just…almost.

Richard, my stepfather, and Abraham had built a close bond, and since Abraham's return, Richard had become much more involved in our lives. For a long time, I knew Richard had felt guilt over Abraham's absence, and with Abraham's return, his guilt had vanished. Not to mention Richard and his very public liking for Helen, who happened to be Danny's mother.

Speaking of Danny, he and Kimmeh were getting married that day! They both, truly, deserved to be happy. Today was going to change a lot in everyone's lives, as Danny and Kimmeh would be moving out of the Virgo mansion and into their own home. After a long debate, I had finally moved in with Sawyer, and with Kimmeh and Danny moving out, it would make this really large house seem even larger.

Sawyer had been helpful, kind, and very, very, patient with me as we made the adjustment of living together. I was emotional during the time I was making the decision to move out of Richard's house. It was my home, the only home I'd ever known, and it was comfortable. Fearing that Richard would be lonely and unsafe without the watchful eye of myself or the Virgos made me scared. Even though Richard wasn't my birth father, I could still say I was a daddy's girl. Through thick and thin, Richard and I had only had each other for the longest time, and even though we didn't get along all the time, the moment I chose to leave made me sad because things would be changing once again. But I knew, in the end, it was the right decision for me. I was growing up. With my light, I had plenty to learn about, and Abraham was there to help me through it. I couldn't live under the roof of my old life because every bit of me was different. Change was coming, either way, moving out of Richard's house or not.

I stood from the chair I was sitting in and went over to the bed across the way to pick up a dress that was laid out on it. Kimmeh had picked it out when we went dress shopping a couple of weeks ago, and I had to admit it was pretty. It was a floor-length gown in an auburn color that was almost the same color as Kimmeh's hair, with a brown ribbon across the waist. Thankfully it fit like a charm, considering she didn't even have me try it on. I would put a penny on it that she'd had a vision before she even bought the gown.

After taking a long look at myself in the mirror, I turned towards the closet to find my black flats.

"Cameron?" I smiled at the sound of Sawyer's deep voice.

I pulled myself up and pulled the door back a little to peek my head out. Sawyer came up to me from the hall and smiled down at me, holding up a tie. I laughed, stood, and took it from him. After laying it around his neck, I placed it correctly on him, tied it, and then tucked it into his tux before getting a good look at him. He looked fantastic. It was only about a week ago that he had decided to surprise me by cutting off his long sandy hair. The day he got it cut, he failed to tell me because he knew I would protest. Sander and Shane had kept me busy by entertaining me with old photographs of them as children, which included a heartbreakingly sweet photo of Sawyer when he was only three, wearing a diaper, and holding a dinosaur figurine in one hand, and in the other, a red blanket that to this day was hanging on a chair in Sawyer's bedroom. Let's say when I got the phone call from Sawyer, I wasn't entirely happy with him…that was until he showed up, and he looked so handsome I had to let it go. It was short but still long enough for me to slide my fingers through it.

Sawyer went over to the bed and pulled his dress shoes out from under it. He began to place them on as I searched for my flats again.

"It's hard to believe…." I began tugging for my flat that was stuck under a pile of other shoes and junk that I had yet to find a home for, including some paintings and painting supplies. "Kimmeh and Danny are actually getting married," I said, pulling pair after pair of shoes out of the closet.

"Kimmeh is like one of the boys. She always has been. So I must say it's going to be quite a show when I see her in a gown," Sawyer chuckled. After a moment of agitation, I closed my eyes and thought about my shoes, and in only a moment, they appeared in my hands. For almost two months, I had chosen not to use my powers until I finally decided it was time to embrace who I was now. With Abraham's help, it had become a lot easier. "I wish I didn't have to be the one walking her down the aisle, though." I walked over to the bed and sat next to him, then pulled on my flats. "Our father should be the one doing it." I looked over at him. Sawyer rarely talked about his parents, so it took me by surprise when he said that. Actually, he never spoke about them at all. I knew Kimmeh, Sawyer, and Sander were siblings, but none of them ever spoke about their parents. I placed a hand on his shoulder and caressed it before laying a kiss on his cheek. Today would be an emotional day for all of them, I was sure. He grinned at me. "But, I'll make sure to make her happy today."

Gently patting his back, I stood. He looked up at me, taking my hand as he stood too. He spun me around, and

I couldn't help but giggle, letting him lead me around in a small circle. Once I was facing him again, he pushed my hair behind my ear and placed both of his large rough hands on my cheeks. "You better go on and make sure Kim is ready. She'll need you to keep her sane. The clock is ticking fast, Cam, and she needs to be ready by two o'clock."

I had to stand on my tiptoes to give him a kiss, and without hesitation, he kissed me back. After looking at him for a few seconds more, I left the room and went down the hall to where Kim was getting ready. Sawyer went behind me and down the steps, out of my view.

The door opened slowly until an unfamiliar face looked out to me. She had black hair that went down past her waist a little longer than mine, and she was rather short.

"Is Kimmeh ready yet?" I asked, trying to look around her.

"Come on in, Cameron! It's fine, Ashley. She's my maid of honor," I heard Kimmeh say.

The young girl moved from my path as I entered. I came in to find Kimmeh sitting in front of her own mirror, picking at her hair. I smiled at her, shaking my head. "You need to get into your dress, Kim," I said, picking up the gown that was laid out on her bed. She turned to me with a pout.

"Why does it have to be so girly? I like to play in the mud and do things most girls wouldn't…why do I have to do all of this?" she asked, picking at her hair again as she turned back to look in the mirror.

"Because it's what people do when they have a wedding. Just think how Danny is feeling right now. Let's just hope he'll be able to fit into his tux! Sawyer seemed to barely fit in his." Last year Sawyer had been much thinner than the other Were's, but ever since the battle against Collin ended, he'd been trying to get in shape. I tugged on Kimmeh's arm for her to stand. She did as commanded but still pouted. "It's what people expect, you know?" I said as I laid the gown back on the bed to unzip the back. I turned back to Kim and gasped when she let her robe fall to the ground, showing her privates to me. With the girl behind me giggling, I looked away as I laid the gown over her and pulled it down some till her head popped out of the top. She blew at her hair to get it out of her face. "You look perfect," I said, turning her around so I could zip the back. She continued to stare at herself in the mirror. Once I was done zipping up the bottom and tying the lace up her back, I laid my chin on her shoulder to look at her. She looked stunning.

Her auburn hair was pulled up into curls with a simple curl that went down her face — the one she just kept picking at — and her makeup was simple. Her green eyes sparkled as she smiled. "I guess I don't look too bad," she said. I nodded in return. "Oh!" she said, suddenly turning to me. "I am so sorry! Cameron, this is my cousin, Ashley; and Ashley, this is my best friend, Cameron." I smiled at Kimmeh when she said, best friend. I knew for a long time Kimmeh and I had become close but had never actually heard her say we were best friends. It was a good feeling to know that there was someone I could truly trust and admire other than Sawyer.

The same girl who had answered the door looked up from the other side of the room where she sat on a rose-colored chair and answered with a soft, "Hi."

"It's nice to meet you," I returned, smiling at her. Her eyes were large, and her skin was pale, unlike the Virgos, whose skin was tan. Nor were her eyes green, but dark...almost hazel. As it seemed there was no more to say, I looked back to Kimmeh. She looked absolutely spectacular when she was ready. Like a princess about to be crowned.

"Is she a — you know — too?" I asked Kimmeh quietly.

Kimmeh only smiled and wrinkled her nose before replying. "No, she's not." She glanced back at Ashley before leaning into me. "My aunt and uncle, her adopted parents, were killed…along with mine." She went silent for a moment before pulling herself up. "She was raised by our nana, like me and my siblings."

"You have a nana?" I asked, astonished at the idea of Sawyer and his siblings having a grandmother. We had never spoken about it, and it was the first time I felt true sadness for the Virgos. The three, or four, if you included Ashley, had lost their parents at a young age while growing to become werewolves — not including Ashley — and were raised by their grandmother. I had never known either of my grandmothers or grandfathers, as they had already passed when I was born.

Kimmeh coughed a laugh and hugged me. "Of course we have a nana! Who doesn't? You'll meet her, I'm sure…she's with the guests downstairs."

"I'll most definitely have to. Are you ready?" After giving her arm a squeeze and receiving a nod from her, I went to the door and opened it to peek outside and make sure none of the guys were around, most importantly Danny. He should already be downstairs waiting for her, but Danny was the type to come snooping.

"Sawyer!" I said in a heavy whisper. With his amazing were-hearing, I knew wherever he was, he would be able to hear me. It took only a few seconds before he came dashing up the steps from downstairs and then to my side. "She's ready." I stepped from the doorway and let him enter the room.

He stopped in his steps when he saw his sister. Sawyer simply gave her a crooked smile as Kimmeh went over to him and took his arm that was out to her. When they passed me, I gave her a thumbs-up, then grabbed the bottom of her gown so she wouldn't trip over it. Her gown was a simple white with a heart neckline and shoulder straps that hung off the side. It was plain until you reached the waist, where a line of roses dripped down to her train. Once she was far enough, I dropped the train, so it followed behind her.

"You look beautiful, Kim," Sawyer said to Kimmeh, who looked away from him.

"Don't cry now. You'll ruin your makeup!" I said with a laugh. As I turned to return to her bedroom to retrieve my flowers, I almost bumped into Ashley—in an identical gown to the one I was wearing—who was already coming out of the room with the flowers and handed them to me with a smile. I smiled back in thanks.

The music started, and that was our cue to go. With Ashley behind me, we went ahead of Sawyer and Kimmeh, who waited at the top of the steps.

"Cameron!" a voice whispered in a harsh tone. I turned to find Kimmeh staring at me with round eyes. "Ashley, you go on," she said, waving at her cousin to continue down the stairs. Ashley nodded and went on, leaving me behind with Kimmeh and Sawyer, who both were staring at me.

"What?" I asked.

"Your hands! Put them out." I had no idea what she was talking about until I looked down to find that my hands were glowing. There wasn't really a way to just "put them out" like Kimmeh had stated, but I waited a moment, repeating in my mind for them to lighten, and finally, the glow faded from my skin.

"I'm just so happy," I said, and with an apologetic smile, I went down the steps, doing my best to not fall flat on my face. I heard Sawyer chuckle behind me.

When the entrance hall came into view, it was unbelievable. The room was covered in red roses, chairs painted a brown to match the bows of our dresses, and then there was Danny. He was wearing a white tux with a brown tie. He gave me a large smile and practically hopped where he stood, patting his feet against the floor. Sander and Shane stood behind him and waited much more patiently. Shane was grinning as usual, and Sander simply gave me a soft smile and a nod.

Once Ashley and I took our spots on the side, Sawyer and Kimmeh came down the steps. I glanced around at everyone as they stood. I didn't recognize a lot of them but knew a few of Danny's family, including his mother and sister, who were sitting next to my stepfather Richard.

The moment Kimmeh came into full view, I looked over at Danny. In his eyes was love… real unconditional love. This was the only wedding I had ever been a part of other than my mom's with Richard. I didn't remember much about my mom's wedding since I had been so young. But Kimmeh and Danny's was nice, peaceful, and beautiful. After everything I'd put them through, they deserved it.

Sawyer lifted the veil from Kimmeh's face and placed a kiss on her wet cheek as Kimmeh cried softly. She moved to stand beside Danny once Sander and Shane took a step back. I watched as the couple exchanged their vows and then shared their first kiss as man and wife.

Everyone gathered outside for the cake and gifts. Danny splashed Kimmeh with cake and was yelled at by an elderly woman about getting cake on Kimmeh's dress. No one around them could keep their composure, including myself. After the cake, the crowd dispersed to join the party Shane had started on the dance floor.

When I felt a cold hand touch my arm, I turned to find an older woman whose hair was silver and eyes were a dark green. She smiled at me before pulling me into a hug, laughing as she did so. I only patted her back, wondering who she was before she pulled away and placed both hands on my cheeks.

Then I remembered her as the woman from earlier who wasn't very happy about Danny getting cake on Kimmeh's gown.

"You must be Cameron! Sawyer and Kimmeh both have told me so much about you! I'm Neila, their nana." She gave me a very warm smile. "You wouldn't believe how happy I was when Kimmeh told me that Sawyer had finally found someone after such a bad event a couple of years ago. He deserves happiness."

"Bad event?" I asked.

"Oh!" His nana looked down in embarrassment. "Oh dear, it's nothing to worry about." Her face turned from embarrassed to nervous as she finally let my face go and patted my arms at my side.

"What happened?" I asked.

"Where's the champagne? Waiter?" She hurried away from me, chasing down a waiter who had passed.

I began to follow her just as Richard called out to me. I looked towards where Neila had scurried but let it go and walked across the field to Richard, who was now talking with Kimmeh and Danny. With them was Danny's mother, Helen, and his younger sister, Amy. It had been so long since I'd seen Helen, and it felt so right when I reached her and gave her a hug.

My mom and Helen were best friends growing up. I could remember vaguely when my mom passed away that Helen was there almost the entire time, helping Richard with burial arrangements and groceries and doing laundry. Considering Danny had lost his father when he was eight and I was seven, we sorta bonded. I believed it made us stronger. Helen never met Jack, my biological father, because he was never around when we were young and eventually left us altogether. This was the reason I assumed Jack didn't join us at the wedding.

Abraham came over to us with Emily by his side.

"How are you, Cameron?" Helen asked me as she gave Abraham a pat on the arm.

"I'm great, Helen, thank you. How are you?" I asked, smiling at her.

"Exhausted. But I am so happy for Danny."

Sander came up to us, "Sorry to interrupt, but it's time for the gifts. Cameron, could you help me bring some of the gifts over?" Sander asked.

"Yeah, sure. I'll be right back," I told Helen as I turned from her, then crossed the lawn to the house. From the corner of my eye, I saw Sawyer speaking with his nana, who was now drinking from a full champagne glass. He caught my glance and exchanged it with a smile before I went into the house. When reaching the living room, I found the gifts were piled one on top of the other on the other side of the room where the couch had once been. There were a couple of larger gifts, but I went for the smaller ones first.

"I'll take those," Sander said, grabbing a couple of large packages and heading towards the door as if it were nothing.

I began to pick up a few of the smaller gifts as something caught my eye. I had to reread the envelope four times before it sunk in. Gavin Montue. The envelope read Cameron, and it was taped to a gift for the wedding party.

"Coming?" Sander asked me.

I looked back at him. "I'll be heading that way," I said. After Sander left the room, I laid the gifts back down, carefully took the envelope off the gift, and opened it. I pulled the letter out and read:

Cameron,
It's been a while since we've seen each other. I'm sorry it's taken me this long to come in contact with you. We've been busy down this way, and I thought this would be the

best time to write. We're in the States right now visiting with another Were family who is curious about you. It seems everyone knows about the great light carrier now since you took out Collin, and I must say it would be wise to not flaunt your gifts. Believe me when I say Collin wasn't the only one who would love to get their hands on your abilities.

Before I forget to tell you, our bond is now broken. It broke a while back, but, as I said, I've been busy and wasn't able to write to you. Once I have the time, maybe I will call to hear that sweet American voice of yours. Our bond has broken, but our friendship has not.

Tell Kimmeh and Daniel congrats from the Montue Pack!
-Gavin M.

I closed the letter and smiled to myself. I would love to see Gavin again. He had become one of my closest friends in such a short amount of time. Before he left, he told me he was a Protector and that he was meant to protect whoever it was that was bonded to him. It wasn't uncommon for Weres to receive special abilities...they called them "gifts." Just as Kimmeh had visions, Sander and Abigail could heal, Kyle could hear thoughts, and so on. Gavin's gift was different. Unlike the other Weres, his gift couldn't be controlled but was forced through him...a random thing that just took hold of him was how he described it. When he was bonded to someone, he was forced to protect them at all costs, and after his duties were done, he had to leave for their bond to finally break. Had he left me while bonded to me, he would have never been able to forget me. Once he'd explained to me that he felt a strong pain in his heart until he was reunited with the one he was to protect. A tense pain. It was sad, really, how it controlled him. But I also had to think of all the good he'd done by helping people like me. He had kept me sane during the hard times last year. I would never truly be able to thank him for that, especially through a letter.

It would be great to see Rebecca, Tyler, Sam, Abigail, Kyle, and Gavin again. It felt like a century since I'd seen them. Placing the letter into my bag, I picked up the boxes I had set down and took them out to everyone else who was waiting for me.

Later that night, after everyone had left, I sat on the couch in the living room. With tea in hand, I sat and looked at the non-lit fireplace. I smiled up at Sawyer as he joined me.

"What a day," he said, taking a seat next to me.

I nodded, taking another sip of my tea. "You can say that again."

"What a day."

I looked over at him. "I wasn't being serious."

He chuckled, kissing my head. "I know. Come on, let's get to bed."

I drank the rest of my tea before Sawyer took the empty glass from me. I followed him until we reached the steps, where he continued to the kitchen, and I went up the stairs to our room.

I lit a candle next to the window and turned the lights off. After I put on my pj's, I pulled the covers up and laid on my right to look at Sawyer, who entered the room and eventually laid down too. We lay there looking at each other in silence. Last year I had thought that I would never see him again, but here we were, laying in the same bed and loving each other more than ever. I didn't know what I would have done if he had never come back to me. I knew I had seemed selfish back then, with my trying to forget him thing. It had been so painful, the thought of him actually leaving me on purpose. But I knew deep inside he was out there, and the moment I found he was alive, I wanted him back more than ever. I didn't even want to think about how it would have been had Collin succeeded. Collin got what he deserved.

I crawled up to Sawyer and lay my head on his chest. His hand lifted to my hair to gently play with the ends before kissing the top of my head again. We lay there in the dim, silent room until I thought of my hand glowing, and it did so. It had taken me about a month and a half to finally learn to control my light; it hadn't helped when I tried to push it aside and live my life to the norm. But I still had a lot to learn, and Abraham had been there to train me. He'd been a good teacher.

I listened to Sawyer's heartbeat, which beat a lot faster than my own. His breathing was deep and hollow. He placed his hand over my glowing one, picked it up, and placed it to his lips. My lips went up into a smile as he did.

It didn't take long till we both fell asleep.

CHAPTER 2

I woke to find an empty right side of the bed. I sat up, rubbing my eyes and barely letting them open because of the bright light of the sun. Standing from the bed, I took a few steps forward till I got to the mirror and looked at myself. I looked horrible. My hair was every which way, my eyes were pale, and my lips were chapped. Of course, they would chap during the spring. I rubbed my eyes once again.

A buzzing sound caught my hearing, and my eyes snapped to my right to find my phone moving around. I opened it to find a text from Abraham.

I thought we were having practice today? I'm waiting.

I typed back. *Sorry! Overslept. I'll be there in a few.*

Once the message was sent, I quickly went over to the closet and pulled out a shirt and shorts. After getting dressed, brushing my teeth, and throwing my hair into a ponytail, I put my phone into my back pocket and exited the room. Going out the front door, I smiled when my pretty navy blue Jeep came into view. I was so glad when Richard brought my Jeep back to me. I had missed it so much.

I hopped into the vehicle but didn't try to turn the car on. The keys dangled in the ignition as my finger tapped the steering wheel. An odd feeling of uncertainty filled me. I hadn't felt the sensation since the defeat of Collin, and for some reason, a feeling in my bones made me unsure about going to Abraham's.

Emily and Abraham had moved back into his old house, which they'd built back up to its old structure. On the night he and I were chased from the home by Gathiens a few years ago, the home had suffered some damage. Emily wasn't exactly one I would call a friend, as she never stayed in the same room as me for more than five minutes and always tried to cause my lessons with Abraham to be cut short. Kimmeh didn't like her a bit, and I understood why. But Abraham was my brother, and I had to at least try to get along with her even if she didn't want the same with me.

I shook my head and then wiggled my fingers on the steering wheel before I actually took hold of my keys and started the Jeep.

Abraham lived on the other side of town, yet it didn't ever seem to take long to get to his house. When I finally reached it, I went straight to the backyard, where he always waited for me, and just as I expected, he was standing there with a stick in his hand when I reached him at the wood line.

"You going to use that on me?" I joked.

He shook his head and stared at me sternly. "Today, we are going to work on your speed," he said, and in an instant, threw the stick at me quicker than my eyes could see. It hit me square on the chest. With a slight "Oh!" I bent to the ground to catch my breath. "We obviously have a lot of work to do."

"A lot of work to do? You threw it at me before I was even ready! I just got here." I looked up at him as I breathed heavily.

"No one is going to wait till you're ready."

"I don't see why we have to do this. We killed Collin,

so there's no use," I huffed, picking up the stick. Abraham watched me as I did so. Every Wednesday and Thursday morning, Abraham and I would meet at his place to practice. He had many years over me, and it showed every time that he was more powerful than I was. He was faster, stronger, and more intelligent. But I was learning.

I enjoyed our training, really I did, but I always wanted to learn more about our past and what we were. Abraham always used the excuse of not knowing about our past, but I had a deep sense that he knew but didn't want to tell me. The only things I knew about our past were what Abraham told me of what Collin had told him. Collin was apparently our great, great, great, so on and so forth, uncle. He had wanted Abraham and me to be on his side and make the humans bow down at our feet. Honestly, it didn't make any sense to me. How was Collin our uncle? He'd spoken of a woman named Zalvana Peythron, who was supposedly our grandmother who had been with Collin's father. Still, it didn't explain what we really were, only that we were called a mix.

Whack. "Ow! Abraham!" Without even letting me throw the stick back, he had vanished, got the stick out of my hands, and whacked me on the back of the head with it. Rubbing my head, I glared back at him. "That was uncalled for," I said, crossing my arms defiantly.

"Start paying attention then."

"I am!" I yelled back.

"No, you're daydreaming. I don't know what about, but you're not paying attention to anything I'm saying. What's so important that you aren't paying attention to me?" He crossed his arms too.

"I was just...thinking."

"Thinking about what?"

"Collin and Zalvana."

He sighed. "I've told you many times, there's no way we can truly know if what he said was true or not."

"Yeah, I know, but it just seems weird. The fact he knew all along that we were his family, his blood, and still he tried to force me to be with him. It just doesn't make any sense to me."

"Come on." He lifted his hands up, palms facing me, after dropping the stick to the ground. I pulled mine up, too, towards him. "We may never know whether Collin was telling the truth, and according to Jack, there isn't much to go on at this point. So let it rest for now, and let's practice. Now, remember to always think about what you want to do…otherwise, it won't work as you planned. I want you to think of pushing me to the ground. Don't hesitate, just do it."

I fiddled my fingers some before thinking of Abraham. Thinking of pushing him down. Pushing him to the ground. Warmth came to my palms with a flash of light that went forward towards Abraham and pushed his chest, throwing him backward. With a simple movement of his own hands, he caught himself before he landed. How he could think so fast, I didn't know, but I seriously need to learn how to do it.

Once he got himself situated, he looked at me. "Good job."

"Hey Ab," I said, picking up the stick he had dropped.

"Yeah?" he answered as he fixed his shirt.

"I got a letter from Gavin." Still fiddling with the stick, I kept my eyes focused on the ground.

"The foreign? What did he have to say?"

"He isn't just 'that foreign,' Ab; he also happens to be a good friend," I snapped. "He told me our bond is broken now, so he can probably call me or even see me!" I quickly threw myself from his power. Abraham vanished and then reappeared next to me, putting a hand out to help me to my feet.

"First, he tells you he can never see you again, and now all of a sudden, a year later, he wants to pick up where you two left off? What does Sawyer have to say about that?"

"I haven't really spoken to him about it yet...."

"You may want to before he finds out you've kept this from him. He's protective of you. I can see it."

"I know," I said, a little annoyed. "I will."

Abraham's face turned, and his lip quivered slightly as if in thought. I watched him and was about to ask what he was thinking before he opened his mouth. "Actually, Cam, there's something I'd like to talk to you about since we're talking about our personal lives."

"Shoot."

We sat next to each other on the ground. It must have been important if he wanted to stop training and take a seat. I would probably need to brace myself. I looked over at him. He seemed so deep in thought I didn't want to say anything. I'd give him time, space to think of what it was he really needed to talk to me about. Finally, he looked over at me with a serious look.

"Am I getting old?" he asked.

This wasn't what I'd expected to come out of his mouth. I didn't even know what to say as I stared at him. I burst into laughter, having a hard time controlling myself. His face kept still. Was he old? He didn't look any older than about twenty. Abraham was a few years older than me, I knew, but he wasn't old. I was nineteen, he was twenty-three now — but not in appearance — and twenty-three wasn't old. At least not to me. Letting the laughing ease, I looked at him, shaking my head.

"Well, you've been stuck in your nineteen-year-old form for years. So I would say you're young...but then again, your appearance is different than your actual age...." Where was I going with this? "All right, for argument's sake, you are *very* old. Why?" I laughed again.

He shook his head. "No, no. Would I be too old to still be able to have a family of my own? Even if I'm not able to have children, I think adopting would be nice someday."

This was surprising. "Adopting? With who?"

"Emily, of course. We talked about it a few nights ago, and she spoke about how her family had adopted many kids. Neither of us is capable of having children since our change — at least, I know she isn't able — but I think giving her children would be a good thing. I would like to marry her, Cam. But I...," he said before looking at me, "I need your consent."

"My consent? Why mine? You're the older brother."

"I know. But you mean a lot to me. Your opinion matters."

"Well, I don't really know Emily that well. Ever since you both came back, she really hasn't had much to say to me or even tried to get to know me. You were taken from me when I was fourteen, and I just feel like we really haven't had enough time together before you decide to get married and run off —"

"I've been back over a year."

"Still. Don't you think it's a little too soon?"

"I've been half dead for years; 'a little too soon' doesn't go with me."

"You'll just have to let me think on it."

"That's all I ask."

"Abraham!" Emily yelled from the house.

I looked up to her, then back to Abraham, whose eyes widened as he looked to Emily. He looked defeated as if she had an invisible leash wrapped around his neck. Usually, he would never even give a girl a second glance, and here he was totally oblivious of me being there even after we were just talking. He nodded to her in response, and I felt my shoulders slump.

"We can continue some other time," he said softly.

"But we just started!" I said, looking up at him as he stood.

"I know, but…we just need to continue another time." He hurried up the hill to meet Emily.

"Yeah, sure, why not."

Emily sure had him wrapped around her little finger. This wasn't exactly a good start on me agreeing with him marrying Emily. Even in a year's time, I had only spoken to Emily a few times. She was very private and never wanted to go out when we invited Abraham to our get-togethers at the Virgos. I had yet to get a good vibe from her. Then again, who could blame me? She was a part of that horrible gang that had stolen Abraham from me all those years ago.

I stood and followed Abraham's steps up the hill. As I came up to them, I heard Emily speaking. "I woke up, and you were gone," she said as they walked towards the house. Her fingers were entwined in his hair.

"Sorry, I left a note on the refrigerator," Abraham replied.

"Well, what did the famous Cameron say?" Emily asked, eyeing me when I walked up to them to head towards my Jeep.

The famous Cameron? Was she seriously saying that? I was his sister! Looking her up and down, I bit my lip, hard enough to cut through it, then had to lift my hand to check for blood. I grunted when I found a red smudge.

"'scuse me. I'll talk to you later," I mumbled to Abraham as I hurried past them to my Jeep. Emily laughed behind me. Way to go, Cameron. Way. To. Go.

Kingsley greeted me with a water in hand when I parked the Jeep outside of the Virgo mansion. "How did you know I would need a water?" I asked as we entered the house and proceeded into the kitchen. He walked over to the cabinet, pulled down a box of napkins, and handed a few to me. I wiped off my lip before taking a sip of the water, letting the taste of copper fill my mouth.

"He didn't. I did." I turned to find Kimmeh leaning up against the counter, an apple in hand. She smiled at me. "You really should stop biting your lip. It's a nasty habit, and you wonder why you always complain about having parched lips. It's your own fault, you know."

I smiled at her in return. "It's just a little habit. I do it without even realizing I am most of the time. It's not something I can just stop doing." I went over to her and gave her a hug. "I thought you and Danny were already gone."

"We went home instead and missed our flight."

"You horrible thing," I laughed, nudging her. She shook her head at me.

"Now Cameron, you know me better than that. We didn't do anything...we simply fell asleep and missed it."

"Mhm. I'm sure that's how it went. Have you gotten any more complaints from your neighbors?"

"No." She laughed and looked into the living room before returning her gaze to mine. "You aren't going to actually tell Abraham it's all right to marry her, are you?" she whispered.

Why didn't it surprise me that she knew what had happened at Abraham's? She just had to have visions about everything. "I'm not sure." I took another sip of my water. "I don't really know her, she's never around, and besides...did you notice the sarcasm she had towards me? No wonder I bit through my lip." I lifted the napkin to my lip again.

"Oh, I noticed...which is why I asked." She took another bite of the apple.

"I don't know. Maybe I'm just jumping to look at the cover and not actually taking the time to read the book?"

"I don't have to read it. She has some stained pages.

There's just something not right about that chick."

"King?" I asked. Kingsley looked up to us from the dishes he had been washing. "Have you learned anything about Emily?"

"Abraham's girlfriend? Well, no, actually. She's not around long enough for me to get to know her. Why do you ask?"

"Just asking."

"Cameron doesn't trust her, just like I don't," Kimmeh said.

I glared at her. "That's not true."

"It so is. She aggravates you, I can tell!"

"Aggravation and not trusting someone is totally different, Kim."

"Maybe, maybe not. But I still say we should do some research," she said, throwing the apple core into the trash.

"You can't. You and Danny are leaving, remember?"

"Doesn't mean I can't do some research. Don't worry, Cam, me and Danny have the rest of our lives together. A little time for you won't harm anything." A little time for me...I sighed. Why did it always come back to me? They needed time to themselves. It was their honeymoon time, for lord's sake. She looked up at the clock above me. "I have to head back. Thanks for the apple, Kingsley." She gave me another hug. "Keep in touch. I'll have my phone on me the whole time."

"All right. Bye, Kim."

"Bye!"

She left the room, and in a few seconds, the front door opened and closed.

"It's going to start getting lonely around here, Kingsley," I said.

"Perhaps then I'll be able to retire," he said with a laugh, and I joined in.

The front door opened again and then shut, and shortly Abraham and Emily joined us in the kitchen. As Abraham made his way towards me, she stayed in place.

"Ah, Mr. Evans! Will you be staying for lunch today? I was just prewashing the dishes from this morning's breakfast."

"Thank you, Kingsley, but we must be heading out soon. I just stopped by to give Cam this." He handed me a picture, and I looked down at it in amazement. My eyes lifted to him, then fell back to the photo.

"Where did you find this?"

"I found it in the attic. I forgot to give it to you when you came over. I made a copy for myself."

I hugged him. It was a family photo of me, Abraham, Richard, and Mom. In the photo, both Richard and my mom were looking straight at the camera. My mom was in a long white gown that showed her bare shoulders, and Richard wore a white tux. It was their wedding photograph. Abraham stood next to Mom, almost hiding behind her, as I held onto Richard's hand with a thumb in my mouth. I had to have been at least three, and Abraham around seven or eight.

As Abraham was pulling from me, I could have sworn I saw Emily's eyes glare at us as she took hold of Abraham's arm and pulled him back. Had I done something wrong to make her mad at me? Being the girl that I was—ugh—I glared back at her in spite when Abraham and I pulled apart.

"Why are you looking at her that way?" Abraham blurted.

I looked up at him in surprise. "Looking at who what way?" I asked.

"Emily. Why are you glaring at her?"

"I wasn't the one who started the glaring…she did! I was glaring at the eyes that were glaring at *me*." That didn't make any sense. Jeez. Abraham looked at Emily and moved from my view so I could see her too. Her looks had completely changed back to their normal state…innocent. What was with girls lately? I couldn't even hug my own brother without a girl getting pissed.

"Apologize," Abraham said to me…to me! She was the one glaring at me, and I was having to apologize? "Apologize!" This time when he said to apologize, he said it in an angry tone.

"I'm sorry that you were glaring at me first, Emily," I said. My hand instantly lifted to my mouth with shock. I didn't mean to say that out loud. "No! That's not what I meant!" I said.

"It's exactly what you meant. Come on, Emily, let's go."

Abraham took Emily by the arm to lead her from the room, and as Emily was turning to leave, she gave me the stink eye. That girl must have issues. At first, she seemed nice and like a sweet little pumpkin pie, but apparently, I was way off. She was with Collin way longer than she was around Abraham…maybe she had been too deeply into it. I didn't know. But there had to be something going on that I didn't know about. Was she trying to get between me and my brother? To keep him for her own? That would be so stupid. And now Abraham wanted me to tell him I thought it was a great idea to marry her. I didn't really know her, but from the few times I'd met her, she didn't seem too fond of me. Maybe Kimmeh had an idea….

"I saw it too," I heard Kingsley say. After putting my bottle into the trash, along with the tissue I had used, I left the room.

I climbed the stairs slowly, trying to figure out what had happened in there. Was I just letting Kim get to me about Emily? Or was I seeing Emily's true colors? With Kimmeh and Danny gone, Sander never being home, and Shane gone as well, the house was quiet. I entered my room that was empty, just as it had been this morning. I felt my lip again to check for blood, and gladly there wasn't any. I stood there for a moment until two bold hands went around my hips. I looked to them with a smile before looking up to find Sawyer looking down at me.

"You have no idea what kind of a morning I've had," I told him.

He chuckled. "There's never a day that you don't have something to tell me about. But I have something that might make your day better."

"What is that?" I asked.

A small square nudged me from his jacket pocket. So many things rolled through my mind about what it could be — my dumb short attention span. Sawyer didn't answer me but went over to the bed and sat down. He patted an empty spot next to him, signaling for me to sit. I did so, and he pulled the small box out of his jacket and held it up towards me. I took it with nervous hands, looking at the box and then at him, and waited a moment for him to say something. Oh my full moon, he was going to propose! When he didn't say anything, I went ahead and opened the box.

My smile weakened a little when the present came into view. It wasn't a ring, but a necklace. I looked at it and was amazed after I realized what it was. It was almost an exact replica of the necklace Sawyer always wore around his neck. Shaped like a teardrop, the top edge wasn't even with the pointed top, and an inner trail followed the inside of it on the left, with an open circle in the center. It was like everyone else's, except Sawyer's. All the Virgos had one. Sawyer's, however, was the opposite. His uneven edge was on the opposite side, just like the inner trail, and the circle was filled in.

He pulled it out of the box for me and held it out to put it around my neck. After he tied it on, I lifted my hand to feel it. I didn't know what it was, but the moment his hands dropped from the necklace, something inside of me sparked, like I had just licked my finger and placed it in a socket. Sawyer seemed to have noticed, and his grin went into a large smile.

"What?" I asked with a slight laugh, looking at him.

"Did you feel anything?" he asked.

"Was I supposed to?" I asked, and he nodded in return. "Yeah, I did."

"And you don't know what that means, do you?"

"Not a clue."

Sawyer moved closer to me in a hop like a child. I laughed a little at him as he pushed my hair from my face and behind my ears. "That was the sign of acceptance. You are officially a Virgo. The first time ever that a Gathien mix and a Were have bonded together." I rubbed the necklace again with a thin smile. "You're also mine. I've waited for you for so long."

"I thought I was already yours," I said with a grin.

"You are." He leaned in and gave me a kiss. "You just are more officially mine, I guess."

"Because that makes complete sense," I said, pushing his hair back.

He rubbed the back of his neck with an embarrassed grin. "Are you happy?"

"Very."

CHAPTER 3

Two days later.

Richard

"I think it will be better for the both of you to move to a new place when you feel up to it, Helen. Danny's just moved out. You needn't rush it," Richard said as he placed another full box into his truck. Helen pulled her graying hair back into a ponytail then fanned herself. They had been packing, loading, and unpacking all day. "You both could, maybe, move in with me if you wanted to."

The moment Danny moved out into his own home to live with Kimmeh, Helen had wished to move from their house because of sad memories. Helen explained to Richard that the house belonged to her deceased husband and that she didn't feel right keeping it as her own when it wasn't hers at all.

"That's exactly why, Richard. With Daniel gone, this house is even bigger, with empty spaces and rooms. It's the quietness of it. Amy can have a bigger room where we are moving, and she's just turning sixteen, so it'll be a big thing for her to have her own room…a bigger room. I appreciate your concern, but I think it's time for me and Amy to spend some quality time together. At least I'm going to try. I'm rather excited to move into our new home. Daniel is supportive of my decision, and Amy's excited too."

They both reentered the nearly empty house. Richard picked up a large box near the entrance as Helen picked up two smaller ones. "How is Amy? I haven't seen her since the wedding," Richard asked.

"She's been doing a lot of practicing at the dance school. She's taken on ballet," Helen replied, following Richard to his truck once again.

"Ballet? Well, that will suit her well. Is she dealing okay with Danny moving out?"

"I suppose." She placed the boxes into the back of the truck as he did. "But she's in that stage where it's 'uncool' for a mother to get into her 'business.' Like she has any business at sixteen. She's ready to have a bigger room and more privacy. But we'll see about the privacy thing."

Richard chuckled at her. "I remember when Cameron hit that age. It seems like just yesterday we went out to buy that Jeep of hers. 'All I want is a Jeep, and it has to be blue, or I won't drive it,' she said to me." He chuckled again at the memory. "Don't take offense to anything she says...I'm sure you went through the same thing at that age." They went back to the house to retrieve the last of Helen's things.

"I was taught to behave myself. I was too lenient with Daniel and Amy."

"No, you are a good mother, just as Jules was."

"Jules...." Helen said, wiping off her sweat with her elbow as she went out the front door towards Richard's truck, with Richard following. "Never a day goes by that I don't miss her."

"I still go home thinking she'll be in the kitchen cooking dinner," Richard admitted to her, laying two boxes in the back of the truck. He turned back to Helen, took the two boxes she held and placed them in the back as well. Helen looked at him with sadness, then rubbed his arm in comfort. "She's waiting for me, you know, just as Alan is waiting for you."

"Yes, I know." After patting Richard's arm, Helen headed back into the house. Richard followed a moment later.

Emily

She stomped her foot hard as she threw things across the room. "I don't see why she hates me so, Abraham! I am so kind to her!" she yelled, throwing yet another shoe at Abraham, who bent towards her with sympathy. "Tell her to apologize like a civilized person, and what does she do? She insults me!"

"I told you she didn't mean it. I knew that, but I was so angry at the time I didn't think about it. Truly, Cam wouldn't hurt anyone intentionally."

"And I would? She tried to make me look like a...a... bitch! A bitch, Abraham!"

"Come on, Emily, you're not a bitch, and you know it."

"Of course I know it. I'm not a bitch...I'm much more than that."

"More than that?" Abraham asked.

Emily turned to him, and with a wave of the hand, Abraham was thrown across the room. In a daze, he looked up at her as he slumped to the ground. With a smile, Emily went up to him. She raised her hand and whispered soft words till Abraham's eyes closed in a trance. She let her hand fall to her side as she pulled her shirt down and straightened herself.

"You're getting the hang of things, I see."

She turned to find Shaven, Collin's once right-hand man, leaning against the window sill, his thick body wrapped in a cloak. Her eyes studied him as she licked her lips. "I am." She lifted her eyes to look at his. Within a blink of an eye, he was in front of her. His hands lifted to her head, without touching her, but traced her all the way down to her hips, where he took hold of her and pulled her to him. They kissed deeply. His hand slid up her thigh and then to her hips again, where he began to lift her shirt, but she pulled away, nipping at his lower lip, "Not yet, Shaven." She pulled her hair down from the ponytail and looked down at the sleeping Abraham. Shaven looked also with a strong gaze.

"Have you found out any more information?" Shaven asked.

"None. I am over trying to get along with these people. It's been a year, and still, I haven't got any information that's even close to being useful. Even when I have Abraham in a trance, all I get is a name. Zalvana Peythron. He goes on about his father, Jack, and then mumbles the name Zalvana. Nor is Jack very helpful. Only thing new is something about a journal. Have you heard anything from the other covens?"

"Yes, and the Zalvana Peythron, she's filth," Shaven spat.

"How so?" Emily asked in interest.

"According to some, she was the last woman to wed your father. Obviously, the woman told your father, Gaspard, she was of pure Gathien blood, but she wasn't at all. Are you sure your father never told you of this?" Emily shook her head at him. "She was a spirit, a creature of light. No one truly knows exactly what she was, but she gave birth to a child. Legend says the moment the baby came out, its whole body glowed. Your father thought it was a fascinating power until he found that it wasn't a power at all but that Zalvana was not a Gathien. She had used him to create a halfling, to create something powerful to take down the Gathiens."

"She would sleep with a Gathien to take them down? What a slut...but I think I like her."

"You wouldn't like her if you had known her then.

Tretcher, of the Alaskan coven, who knew your father, said Collin was the only son of Gaspard at the time until he found another Gathien woman who gave him more children, including you."

"Only a Gathien with great power would be able to conceive a child. I never questioned it before," Emily said, sitting on the bed near him. "Collin was a terrible brother. He told me nothing."

"Gaspard was very powerful. The older you are, the more powerful you become. He was capable of having children."

"So did he kill this Zalvana?" Emily asked.

"He did. The moment he found out what she was, he destroyed her."

"And the child?"

"Disappeared," he said bluntly.

"Disappeared?"

"He went to kill the child also, but when he arrived at the child's room, the child was gone. Nothing of the child's was left. Not even a doll or the carriage."

"Someone smuggled the bastard child out."

"I would say so. Wait...." Shaven's eyes snapped to Emily's.

"What is it?" she asked. "Spit it out!" She stood from the bed.

"Isn't this one of light?" he asked, pointing at Abraham. "And his sister?"

"I wouldn't say of light, but they do have special abilities. Why?" she asked curiously.

"Zalvana Peythron was of light." He bent over to get a closer look at Abraham. "You don't think they could be true descendants? Could what we're looking for belong to them?" He looked back at Emily.

She thought about it for a moment. "Yes. Collin should

have told me these things before he got his ass killed. But I found this out myself. I have new questions to ponder." She smirked up at Shaven, who returned it with a grin. "Place this around his neck," she said, handing a gold chain to him. He looked at her in question but didn't speak, then took it from her and placed it over Abraham's neck and tied it to the chair. It pierced his skin with a sizzle.

"Very nice," Emily said as she turned from the two. She went over to the opposite side of the room and pulled a picture from the wall. She looked at it for a long time before she closed her eyes. She began to transform. Her height expanded, her hands and feet grew, and her hair shortened and greyed. Her eyes opened as she turned to look at Shaven, who folded his arms like a warrior.

"So, how do I look?" Emily asked.

"Hideous," Shaven said, snarling his lips in disgust.

"Good. Now that we have a start, fetch me his phone."

Shaven did as she said, going through Abraham's pockets, and after finding his phone, he then handed it to her. She opened it and found the number she was searching for. She waited as it rang. "Hello?" Answered a deep but scratchy voice.

"Hello, Jack! Sorry to disturb you. But, I have some questions to ask you if you have the time," Emily said, with a deep voice that was fairly familiar to her.

"Ah, hello, Richard! Yes, that's fine. What is it?"

"Thanks." She gagged at herself. "I'm having a hard time coming to terms with Cameron and Abraham, and I would really appreciate some advice if you have the time."

"I don't think I would be of much help considering. I'm actually out of town right now paying some bills, but I was still planning on coming over in the morning to use your tools while you're at work. Is that still okay?"

"Oh, yeah, of course."

"All right, and we can have some beers and watch the football game that night. How's that?"

"Sounds good to me. I'll see you then." She hung up. "How was that?"

"Freakishly perfect."

Suddenly there was a banging noise coming from downstairs, and Emily instantly took hold of Abraham's body.

Cameron

I lay on Sawyer's chest as he lay straight on the bed. "I feel bad about what I said to Emily and Abraham," I said, without looking at Sawyer. He didn't say anything to me but laid his hand on my shoulder, pulling with a little pressure before letting it free. "I'm gonna call him and apologize." I got up from the bed, went to the dresser, and picked up my phone before dialing Abraham's number. I called him three times, but no one answered, and it went to voicemail after the third call. I looked at Sawyer in defeat.

"Give it some time. It'll blow over," Sawyer said to me, rolling over in the bed.

I shook my head. "It won't. Abraham won't forgive me." Sitting back on the bed, I looked at Sawyer, whose back was now facing me. "This morning, Abraham asked me to think about blessing him and Emily to be married. Today was supposed to be a good day, and I ruined it by lashing out at Emily. I hate to say it, but maybe I'm jealous. Jealous that she's going to take away my brother, who I've hardly had the chance to see since he came back into my life. I feel like she's taking him from me."

Sawyer looked at me then. "Cameron, I know Abraham loves you. He wouldn't have asked for your blessing if he didn't. He will forgive you, as I'm sure Emily will."

"I need to go see them and tell them both I'm sorry."

"If you feel you have to. I won't stop you from doing what you wish."

I gave Sawyer a soft kiss before getting up from the bed and grabbing my shoes that were next to the bedroom door.

CHAPTER 4

Cameron

"You sure you don't want me to go with you?" Sawyer asked as he followed me from the house.

I opened the Jeep door and crawled in. His face was filled with worry, making his eyes slant down. I couldn't help but smile at him. Ever since he came back, he'd been stuck to my hip, like he was afraid I'd never come back. I'd always come back to him...he was my world. Not many people knew how I really felt about him—"many people," meaning Kimmeh, who knew everything. I put my hand out to him, and he put his face into it, letting me rub his cheek.

"I'll be fine. Really. I just need to go apologize to Ab and Emily. Even though I don't like Emily right now, it doesn't mean I shouldn't at least stay on Abraham's good side." I kissed his forehead then shut the door. "He isn't answering his phone. I'll text you when I get there." Sawyer stepped away from the Jeep as I backed out. With a swift wave to him, I drove down the long road toward Abraham's.

The drive was peaceful. The past couple of weeks had been crazy with the wedding and everything, and it had been hard to have a peaceful moment to myself. I knew what I'd said to Emily wasn't good, trust me, but it had felt so good saying it. Was that bad? I mean, I didn't really know her like Abraham did, but it was like there was something she was hiding. Something I needed to find out before something bad happened to my brother or anyone else. Something deep down inside of me felt she wasn't to be trusted. I had to trust my instinct. I had to keep my brother safe. Emily knew Collin way longer than she had known Ab, and she had even helped Collin find him in the first place. What I didn't understand was, why didn't they take me too? I might have just been overthinking this...I didn't know.

I arrived at Ab's house and got out of the Jeep. The house looked empty, but I went to the front door anyway. When I reached it, I pulled my hand up to knock, but I couldn't get my hand to do it. It was like my hand was cramped shut and wouldn't move for me...it was that sense of uncertainty again. In that instant, my eyes caught sight of a moving figure through the side window next to the door. "Hello?" I called, placing my numb hands against the window and looking in. It was then that I knocked. No one came to the door. Was I imagining things?

No, that was crazy. There was something in there. Someone. I knocked again. "Abraham?" I called. I squinted my eyes to look deeper into the house, and shock went down my spine when the figure looked out from the corner. It couldn't be...no, he was dead! We killed him. Sander killed him. I banged on the door then, and the figure disappeared. "Abraham!" I backed away from the door and held my hands out. *Think only of the light.* Light burst through my palms, light to knock down the door, and it did so. I hurried in, looking around for the figure.

"What the hell are you doing, Cameron?" I turned to find Abraham running down the steps towards me. Of course,

Emily was right behind him in a towel. Water dripped from both of them.

"Her! She's still in contact with those Gathiens! Shaven... he's...I saw him!" As always, my mouth started before I was even aware of what I was doing. I looked to Emily, whose face hadn't changed a bit. Abraham didn't look back at her but kept looking at me. What was she doing to him? "Come on, Ab, you're coming with me." I reached for him, but he pulled away.

"Excuse me? I'm not going anywhere with you." The way he said *you* scared me. His eyes had crossed like I'd never seen before. My eyes studied him, looking for anything else that might have changed about him. I was right. Scars went over his wrists and neck. Was she torturing him?

I'd kill her.

"What are you doing to my brother?!" I yelled at Emily. She simply smiled. "There are scars all over his body, and you can't tell me he did that to himself. What is your problem? Who are you really?" I asked, taking a step forward.

"My, Cameron, nothing gets past you, does it?" Emily finally spoke. Her words were knives.

"You're twisted. Whatever you have over him, set him free, or I'll have to—"

Emily threw her hand up, throwing me back. I let out a yell of pain when I slammed against the wall. My head banged up against the coat hangers before my body slumped to the floor under me. I held my head as it pounded in pain. I looked over to Abraham, whose eyes were now blank as if he were gone and no soul was present. "Come on, Ab, it's me, Cameron. I'm your sister. Look at me!" I pushed myself forward and lifted my hands to him, but I was thrown back again. And I was hit again, and again.

It took me a moment to realize I was in the living room

now as I tried to stand up. I lifted my hands at Emily when she entered the room. She circled me, still holding the towel to her body, and I kept my eyes locked on her, my hands raised, ready to attack.

"Are you really going to try using your itty bitty glow on me, Cameron? It won't work."

"You are really naïve, aren't you?" I asked, feeling my ribs crack inside me.

"Just more powerful than you," she hissed.

"So it isn't about Abraham. It's about me."

"No. It's much more than that." She was much quicker than I was as she threw her hand up like she was swatting a bug. My whole body lifted. Her eyes turned a deep red as she watched me, and my body was thrown back once again, but this time I went out the window. Darkness.

Sawyer

He looked down at his watch, looked out the window, then back to his watch once again. Quickly he took out his cellphone and flipped it open. No calls. No texts. It had been almost three hours since she left the house, and the sun was going down. He dialed Cameron's number once again, but as it had done many times before, it went to voice mail automatically.

"Got in contact with her yet?" Sander asked from across the room as Sawyer closed his phone. Sander and Shane were playing cards on the floor near the fireplace. Sawyer turned to them, shaking his head. "Think we should go see what's going on?" Sander asked again, looking up from the card game that Shane was winning blissfully.

"If we go over there and everything is fine, she will be angry with me."

"But what if something has happened and we don't go

over there? Didn't she say Emily was acting strange?" Sander asked.

"Me and Sander will go then. You'll have nothing to do with it. I've never trusted that Emily girl anyway. Redheads, they kill me. Remember Naomie, my ex-girlfriend from Tennessee? She was crazy," Shane said with a shudder.

"No, if you all go, I'll have to go too," Sawyer replied with a rough snap as he rubbed his short hair. He was still not used to the shortness of it. It had been a bad idea to get rid of it, but it had seemed like a good idea at the time. "Fine," he sighed. "Let's go."

"All right then." Sander picked up the cards, placing them into a small white box. They left the house in a hurry and went to Sawyer's truck. Sawyer got into the driver's seat and Sander in the passenger's, with Shane between them.

When they arrived at Abraham's home, they found glass scattered all across the lawn. Upon exiting the truck, Sawyer transformed into his Were form and entered the house as Shane followed. *I should have known to not let Cameron come alone*, Sawyer thought. Sander stayed behind to look around the outside of the house. Quietly Sawyer crawled up the stairs, taking in any unusual smells. Sensing no one else present, he transformed back into his human form. He looked back at Shane, who crawled up behind him and whose shoulders shifted with confusion.

After finding nothing else out of the ordinary inside, Sawyer and the others went to the truck again. He checked his phone, which still showed no calls or texts. He called Cameron once again.

"Hello?" she finally answered.

"Cameron! Thank God. Why haven't you been answering your phone?" Sawyer asked. Shane and Sander stared at him.

"I went to Richard's, and my phone died, so I used his

charger to charge my phone. Gladly his phone was the same type as mine. Otherwise, I wouldn't have been able to see how many times you'd called me. Why, is something going on?"

"You couldn't use Richard's home phone? I was worried sick that something had happened to you. What happened to Abraham's front window?"

"Sorry, jeez. I don't know, what happened to their window? It was fine when I left."

"It's shattered completely, with glass all over the front lawn. Did you see him before you left?"

"Oh, yeah, we settled things, and we're fine. Is anyone there right now?"

"Not that I can see."

"Well then, I'm sure everything is just dandy. I'm fine."

"Well, just call me when you're heading home, okay?"

Emily

"Okay! Bye." She hung up the phone. With an evil grin, she looked over at the now conscious Cameron, who was held down with gold chains. Abraham sat next to her, covered in chains as well. Cameron shifted in her spot, trying to get at Emily, but a soft grunt exited her mouth from being unable to speak. Cameron's eyes looked to Abraham, who didn't share her glance. His eyes were shut. This only made Emily laugh. "Don't even try to talk telepathically with him...it won't work. You see these chains...they are bonded to myself and Collin. Yes, Collin. My dishonorable twit of a brother. They can chain down any creature we desire." She lifted her hand and waved it towards Cameron, whose face began to shrink then shift. In only moments Cameron was Emily, and Emily was Cameron. In appearance. Shaven walked in with stacks of paper that he laid on the floor. He looked up at Emily, and when he did, his face turned downward in disappointment.

"I can never say enough how much I like your red locks better."

"Is it really so obvious?" Emily asked back with a sneer.

"No. I just know you better than anyone else. Those mutts will believe it, no doubt."

"Good."

"Y-yu carn't do thisss...," Cameron hissed under her breath. Emily turned to her but wasn't fazed at all by her attempt.

"Close her ears, Shaven, we need to talk." Shaven went over to Cameron and placed his hands over her ears. After he released her, she looked at them blankly as he did it to Abraham as well. "Can they hear?"

"Not a word."

Cameron

It all made complete sense...Emily and Collin were siblings! My heart was beating hard and fast as if I had been running for hours. I had to get to Sawyer and let him know. How could they be so stupid? I could hear everything they were saying. I didn't know what these chains were, but they were burning my skin so deeply I could almost see the lift of my skin where it deepened to my bone. *Abraham.*

"But Collin was known back then, and I wasn't. They wouldn't know who I was if we reached it. If I could find a way to go to the past, that would fix everything. It's not too much of a stretch. The other night when we entered Jack's mind, he spoke of a journal that was given to him by his wife. If I found someone to cast an enchantment, maybe we could use it to our advantage. I would need you to stay here for damage control and watch that runt over there, so she doesn't find a way to get back to her little Were friends. We obviously have no way of finding that journal without Jack's help."

Emily's voice went silent.

"Jack only spoke of a journal. Not even Abraham knows of it. We have a great advantage over them, as you said," Shaven said deeply.

"If the stories are true, I want that journal desperately. We won't know the truth about them until we find it," Emily told Shaven. I tried to make myself look like I couldn't hear them. What was this journal they were talking about? Why would Jack know about it? If Jack did have it, I needed to get it first. *Abraham, can you hear me? Answer me.*

"Once you get Jack to speak, he'll be able to tell you more. He's been studying his lives history for years now. We have to be right about them, and if they are the descendants, why doesn't Jack have the same powers as them?" Shaven asked.

"He fought off becoming a Gathien because he wasn't in contact with Collin. Gathiens can only become fully pledged if they have a Gathien present. He was away from his kind long enough that he fought the change. Abraham told me this. Besides, it isn't from Jack's bloodline, it couldn't be, so it would only make sense if it was from their mother's. It's all very confusing. But what aren't we remembering?" Emily looked at me. "All these years, and we hardly have anything to go on. Collin can rot in his burned grave. You are right. Jack will know. I better go over and revisit with him." She turned to leave the room. "Watch them like a dog."

"I kill dogs."

"Yes, my sweet, but if you're a dog, she won't run."

AHHH! Abraham screamed at me telepathically. "Ow!" I screamed. He was awake!

I swallowed when Emily turned back to me. Shaven eyed me as well.

"Thank you, Cameron, you just reminded me. Shaven, dear, make sure she learns her lesson about sticking her nose into other people's business." Then she was gone. I looked at Shaven with fear as he picked up a thick...rope? String? He pulled me up by my hair, making me yell in pain. He ripped the gold chains from my neck and wrapped them around my wrists and legs before throwing me to the floor.

"I wanna hear you scream," Shaven said darkly before lifting the rope into the air, and with a swift flick, it hit my back. I felt the sting, then there was pain, and I could feel the blood flowing from my back. *Abraham, please, he's hurting me! Sawyer, where are you?* Another swing. I yelled once again—so much pain.

Sawyer

"She said she was at Richard's," Sawyer said as they entered their mansion. Sander looked back at him after he shut the door. "You think it would be a bad idea to call his house and see if she's there?"

"If you want to be the obsessed boyfriend, then go right ahead. I'll think it's funny when she comes through that door yelling at you for not trusting her again," Sander said. They both went into the living room.

Shane sat himself back on the floor with the cards as Sawyer sat on the chair. Something buzzed within his veins. As his hand lifted to his necklace, his head snapped to the living room doorway. Sander stood at the doorway of the living room, giving Sawyer a wondering look.

"What is it?" Sander asked.

"It's Cameron," Sawyer said in a faint whisper. Sawyer pulled out his cellphone and called Cameron again. This time she answered quickly, and before she let out her first breath, Sawyer spoke. "Cameron, are you okay?"

"Yeah, I'm fine. Why? Do you not freaking trust me?"

"I do. I'm just worried, is all. I—" Inside, he felt a sense of deep pain. He wasn't sure if it was real, but he felt it. Pain. Their necklaces were connecting them to each other, but Cameron sounded as if she were completely okay on the phone.

"Well, I'm fine. I'll be staying here for the night. Don't wait up." She hung up.

Sawyer looked at Sander, shaking his head. Sander had joined Shane and began to play cards once again.

"Well?" Sander asked with a grin as he threw down another card.

"She's…fine," he replied as he looked up at the clock against the wall.

CHAPTER 5

Sawyer

Sawyer slept deeply until his phone rang. Opening his eyes in slits, he looked at the phone to find a number he didn't recognize. Without any hesitation, he took the phone and answered, "Hello?"

"Hi, Sawyer, it's Gavin. Have you looked in tha newspaper recentleh?"

Sawyer's stomach sunk deep within him, hearing the voice of Gavin. "Gavin?" He hadn't heard from him for over a year. "Gavin Montue?" He looked over at the clock next to his bed, showing the time was four in the morning. He hadn't heard from Cameron since six the night before. "No, no, I haven't," he replied as he sat up in the bed and flipped on the table light next to him.

"Rebecca found something interesting on your town's news site. You may want to go look at it."

Sawyer got up quickly and went across the hall to Sander's room. Sander was still up and on his computer, but Sawyer pushed him to get his attention. "Sander, go to <u>Our NC News</u> website," Sawyer said. Sander did as he said, and in only moments the page uploaded, showing large red letters. Fear hit Sawyer. His hand lifted to his necklace as they read. "Files missing? Do you know which ones?" Sawyer asked.

Sawyer put Gavin on speaker. "Look at tha front photograph, Sawyer; wut do ye see?"

Sawyer and Sander each leaned in to look at the photo. Their eyes widened, and they glanced at each other. "That's not even a photograph. It's a painting. Shit, it's of Collin!" Sander blurted.

"Those papers are very old. Sander, ye 'ave tha best eyes, what year does it say at the bottom?" Gavin asked over the phone. Sander looked closely at the painting.

"It doesn't have a year. It's smudged," Sander told them.

"If those were taken from our library, that means Collin lived here before us. That's how he found Abraham and Cameron," Sawyer said.

"Those papers had te be stolen by someone who knew Collin. If I'm right, then Abraham and Cameron could be in danger again. Someone is visiting, and I don think for a good reason," Gavin said. "I know this is very sudden, but we 'ave been keepin an eye on you for a while. And when Rebecca told me what Sander said about this Emily woman, I put it together, and I fear someone could be trying to bring him back," Gavin replied. "Bring Collin back."

"With a simple piece of paper? Some kid might be doing a research paper for school! They just were too lazy to sign them out at the library," Shane said as he joined them in Sander's bedroom. "Why would they take his information anyway?" Sawyer only shook his shoulders.

"Is Cameron there?" Gavin asked.

"No, she's at Richard's," Sawyer said.

"Somethin's goin' on, Sawyer. I feel it. Get 'er 'ome."

"Since when did you start making calls to Rebecca?" Shane asked Sander.

"She's a friend."

"Sure," Sawyer and Shane said at the same time.

"What? She is!"

Danny

It was early, almost nine when he decided to go to the store and buy some ingredients for a nice breakfast for his new wife. Suddenly his eyes flashed down the road as the sense of Kimmeh filled him. The bags he held fell from his hands when he walked out of the market. The necklace around his neck sizzled through him. He ran down the road as quickly as he could without putting on full speed. Their hotel was only a few blocks down, and when he entered, he pushed through the crowd of people till he reached their room on the fifth floor. "Kimmeh, open the door!" he yelled but lowered his voice as people stared at him. He dug into each pocket before finally finding the key in his shirt. He placed it into the lock and pushed the door open to find Kimmeh on the floor lifting herself up. Her eyes shifted from white to their usual green.

"Cameron...Jack...filled with darkness...yelling...call Sawyer." Her breaths were heaving.

"Come now, sit up." Danny slowly helped her to the bed, where he placed an arm around her shoulders. Danny took his phone out and called Sawyer. Once Sawyer answered, he handed the phone to Kimmeh, who took it automatically.

"Cameron! It's Cameron! Something's wrong with her. Find her!" she yelled.

Sawyer

The moment he shut his phone, he left Sander's bedroom and headed for the door. "Something's happening," he said. "First Gavin and then Kimmeh...we need to find Cameron. Get dressed."

After Sawyer and Sander were dressed and ready, they met Shane at the front of the house, exited, and went to Sawyer's truck that was parked near the gate. He'd known something was up by the way Cameron was speaking to him over the phone. She was hiding something from him, something she obviously wasn't going to tell him willingly.

The drive was a quick one, and when he, Sander, and Shane arrived, it was still not yet sunrise as they each went towards Abraham's house in the dark. Cameron's Jeep wasn't parked out front, but still, they got out to check. When Sawyer saw the front door, he didn't even bother to look around this time but instead burst through the front door that was barely hanging on the hinges. The house looked to be in a remodeling state, though it had only been a few days since Sawyer had been there.

"Cameron!" Sawyer yelled. No reply. Shane and Sander went to the living room as Sawyer hurried up the steps. "Cameron, answer me! Shane, go to Jack's and stay there in case she arrives, and call Kingsley!" He pushed the farthest door open when reaching it and looked in. Nothing. He pulled out his phone and dialed in Danny's number, but it was Kimmeh who answered before the first ring was made.

"I think it's Emily," Kimmeh started instantly. "Cameron told me that Emily had been giving her an odd attitude and how she thought that she might want to get between her and Abraham. I feel like such an idiot for not listening to her completely! I knew there was something up with Emily, but I...."

Sawyer rushed to another room and looked in. Nothing.

"There's no sign of anyone. Is Cameron in trouble or not? Are you sure your vision was true?"

"Have my visions ever been wrong? You should know if there's something wrong, Sawyer...you have her bond."

"You're not perfect, Kim, and there's no sign of Cameron or Richard anywhere. I've felt her feelings all night like fire in my lungs, but she would have told me if something was wrong. I'm not going to force her to tell me, but...." He rubbed his temples. "Something tells me you're both just being girls and don't want Emily around. This stress isn't something I need right now. Did you call Gavin?"

"Gavin? No, I haven't. Why? No, that's not important right now! It's not just Cameron who has seen this...even Kingsley saw how Emily acted towards Cameron. I spoke with him last night. She's up to something. Go to Abraham's."

Emily

The next morning the first thing Emily did was visit Jack's apartment, looking like Cameron, and was lucky to find he had kept his word and was supposed to be at Richard's that morning. She would make sure to make an appearance at Richard's that night, but she was eager to see if the journal was at Jack's. After searching the apartment, she came across a notepad on the small round table near the kitchen, with a time and a name written on it...Richard. She took the notepad and threw it across the room before snapping her fingers in frustration. Upon reaching Richard's house, she found that Richard's truck was nowhere to be seen either, but Jack's car was parked at the front of the home. She transformed back into her natural looks. Casting a glance across the land, she found Jack walking, hammer in hand, to a shed not far from the home. Emily went to him quickly, aggravated at the time she had lost searching for this journal. Swiftly she picked Jack up and hurled him across the way and against his car.

"I knew you were trouble. You'll never get what you're looking for, Emily. Cameron is much stronger," Jack said quickly as he took a stand before her. She slapped him.

"You told me about Zalvana, now tell me about that journal. I'm over playing games. A year has been too long. Where is it? A week ago, I wiped away your memories of me, but you told me about a journal. Tell me." She looked into his eyes deeply until they went blank. His mouth moved in awe until, finally, bits of pieces of what seemed to be words spilled out. Before she had used her powers on Jack, and he'd told her of Zalvana. Collin had been no help, and to Emily, he was just as much a traitor as the Virgos and Evans's.

"Zalvana Peythron, one of light, and powerful." He went quiet for a moment before continuing. "My wife's journal, bonded, given to Sawyer, agreement, one year, protection, hidden. Sawyer...."

Emily threw his face from her grasp and hissed with excitement. "Thank you, Jack, you've been most helpful." She took hold of his face once more and dragged him over to his car, then placed him in it. "Give Cameron a message from me, would you?" His eyes opened and were back to their normal blue hue until Emily grasped his neck and his face turned blue once again, and the veins in his body pulsed. "So weak." She snapped her finger and was sitting in Cameron's Jeep that was still parked in front of Richard's where Shaven had stored it. She drove it to Abraham's, and with a bit of shock, she found a truck in front of the home. She knew it well.

Sawyer

"Sawyer?"

Sawyer turned to find Cameron coming to him. She ran at him and threw her arms around his shoulders as he wrapped his long arms around her waist. He let out a breath of surprise but still hugged her tightly before sitting her down and looking her over. He hung up the phone. "What are you doing here?" Cameron asked, looking up at him.

"Kimmeh had a vision, and Gavin called me about Collin, and then I couldn't get in contact with you." He didn't seem to be making much sense. "I panicked. Kimmeh's vision...." Sawyer let her go, then brushed his hair back.

"I was at Richard's, then I came here. I was just out back when I heard your truck pull up. What is with you lately? It's like you don't even trust me."

"I trust you, it's just—"

"It's just you don't trust me, just say it," she snapped, backing away from him. Then she turned on her heel and stormed away from him, leaving him standing there in silence. He shook his head in confusion.

Cameron

Another whip and I'll be a walking slice of meat.

Only a moment later, I felt the slashing pain wash down my back. All night Shaven had struck me, and all night I tried to awaken Abraham from his slumber. Shaven laughed before speaking. "Now, tell me, beautiful," he began as he looked from the door to me, "is it true you are related to Zalvana Peythron?"

"I don't...know...what...you're....talking about."

"Don't play silly, girl. What about you, Abraham? Do you enjoy watching her be whipped? Why don't you tell me? Emily was kind enough to tell me all about Collin's exchange with you on the night he was killed."

"You know...Emily has...a spell on him." I looked over to Abraham, and for a split second, I could have sworn I saw his eye twitch. *Abraham, you need to snap out of it.*

I'm awake. Don't react to me...I have a plan. I'll get us free.

Sawyer

Nothing made sense to him. Cameron had told him

she would be at Richards's but just happened to show up at Abraham's from Richard's when he'd arrived? Why the sudden change in Cameron that made her so hateful? So jumpy? His fingers fiddled on the steering wheel as they drove back to the house, Cameron at his side. Sander drove behind them in her Jeep with Shane. Fear hit him again. His eyes went to Cameron, who looked out the opposite window without a flinch. He looked back to the road and entered the now opening gates to their home. Her story wasn't making any sense.

After they entered the home, Cameron was automatically at the end of the stairs waiting for him. Taking her outstretched hand, he went up to their room with her, where Cameron hurried in front of him. With a sudden stop and turn, she threw herself on him and kissed him deeply, so deeply that he was hardly able to breathe as her tongue entered his mouth. He returned the kiss without hesitation, but his insides were telling him to stop. *Cameron...she's scared.*

She went to see Richard? No, she was at Abraham's house to apologize for her actions and never returned. She had called, yes, but was acting odd. Cameron pulled him to the bed and laid herself down on it, pulling him down with her. She had never kissed him this way before, ever. She didn't initiate sex. She hadn't even nibbled at her lip once. A moan escaped her lips. Cameron didn't do this.

His hand reached her neck and swiftly took hold of it in a tight grasp, pushing into it, and she began to cough. Her hair lightened to red but flashed back to its natural light brown. No, it was Cameron's natural light brown. "Where's Cameron?!" he growled. The face of Cameron flashed from the figure and then switched to Emily. This continued to happen as he stared at her. She said nothing but laughed at him. Her laugh was a chime of bells to his ears. Sawyer kept his grip on her neck, but it didn't seem to hurt her an ounce. Her fingertips traveled up his arms. A slight pain entered him as the image of Cameron came to him. "What is this trick?" he yelled at her, putting all of his pressure onto Emily. Pain raised into his neck and then to his head, forcing his hands to let go of her in a daze. Something hard was thrown at the back of his head, and he was out.

Cameron

Shaven lifted the chain up to me again. Just before I was going to close my eyes, his eyes widened in shock. I looked down at my hand that began to flicker from my natural light tan state to very pale pink. "Emily!" I jumped at Shaven's shriek. In the blink of an eye, he was gone. I did my best to crawl over to Abraham, whose eyes came open. He leaned over and began to try and untangle himself.

"Abraham, we…." My throat tightened. I gasped for air.

"Cameron? What's wrong?" He turned to me. I didn't know what was happening as I did my best to lift my hands to my neck, where I felt a round indent.

"It's Emily." It deepened farther into my airway…I was being choked.

Then it stopped.

CHAPTER 6

Emily

"It's about time," Emily said, pushing the unconscious Sawyer off her and onto the floor. Shaven dropped the bottom of the now broken lamp on the floor next to Sawyer's body. "Not that I didn't enjoy that." She nudged Sawyer as she wiped the side of her mouth as if she had just had a brilliant feed. Shaven's face was stern before he shook his head. Emily shrugged one shoulder, then smirked at him as she glanced down at Sawyer's unconscious body once more. Shaven didn't seem amused.

"You almost got us caught," Shaven said.

"He just kept calling the phone and asking questions. I couldn't just leave it, now could I? I got Jack to tell me what I needed to know. So get over it. Jack said Sawyer was given the journal. When Jack asked the Virgos to keep Cameron safe from the Gathiens, he must have given it to Sawyer so that if we found out about Abraham and Cameron, he wouldn't have it. Collin must have known about this. He knew all of this."

"Then let's get to looking. Stop acting like a tramp and start acting like your title. Don't mess this up," Shaven said to her. Emily looked at him, and as if insulted, gasped towards him and then glared.

"Me mess it up? Who's the one who just knocked out the one person who knew where it was hidden?" she asked with annoyance in her voice.

"Be quiet! There are still others here. It can't be far."

"We've been searching for this for so long. A few more moments won't kill you, Shaven."

Emily turned from Shaven as he pushed Sawyer underneath the bed and explained what had happened at Richard's while she did so. "Abraham told me Collin said he knew of a Zalvana Peythron. But he never gave me the real information. I always knew he was lying to me, but I needed to stay on his good side. But it all makes sense now." The closet was the first place she looked, throwing clothes out of her way and fiddling her long fingernails in the wall panels to see if there was any chance of a hidden pocket in the wall. She even went so far as to get on her knees to pick at the floor. She looked behind herself to Shaven, who was looking through some books. "The journal will have all of the information we need about Abraham and Cameron's past. The only way we can find out how to destroy them once and for all."

"You're sure he said Sawyer had hidden it for him?" Shaven asked.

"Of course, I'm sure. It has to be here somewhere! Just keep looking." They each continued to search.

Even given how long they both searched, it seemed they would never find the one thing they were searching for—the journal of Zalvana Peythron. Emily looked behind each and every painting, photo, and mirror that hung about, but there was still no sign of a journal. Once Shaven finally turned to her, she threw down a frame.

"It's not here, Emily," Shaven said, crossing his large

arms.

"Where else could it be then?" Emily asked, placing a hand on her waist and letting the other hang at her side. "Jack said he gave it to Sawyer to hide."

"Would it be possible for Jack to have given it to Cameron instead?"

"No. Jack said specifically that he gave it to Sawyer, and I believe it's for an important reason, or else Cameron would have been the first person he gave it to. We both know Gavin Montue is gone and can't come back, so he can't have it."

"Or maybe Abraham?"

"Or Abraham...." Emily lifted her hand to her chin, then rubbed the tip of her lower lip with her finger.

"They have to know something. Cameron and Abraham."

"Let's go." Shaven placed his hand out to Emily, who took it. They both darted from the home, leaving no trace behind. It was only a few minutes before their feet were planted on the floor of Abraham's home. Emily moved forward into the room. Cameron was lying on the floor holding her neck, with Abraham looking down at her helplessly. Emily smiled down at Cameron as she bent down to her. She did this before turning her face to Abraham. "I wonder how it is that you've become such a wonderful liar, Abraham."

"I don't know what you're talking about." Abraham gritted his teeth while rubbing Cameron's shoulder.

Emily smirked. "Why don't you tell me where Zalvana's journal is hidden?"

"What journal?" Abraham asked back.

Emily lifted her hand and, with a swift swing, smacked Abraham across the face. Cameron let out a yelp, catching Emily's attention. Each of the women looked at each other in silence until Emily spoke again, turning her face back to Abraham, who was rubbing his cheek. "Let me be specific.

What is Zalvana to you? We know that both of you are something entirely different...." She eyed Cameron for a second before returning her gaze to Abraham. "Than a simple Gathien. Who is she to you? And tell me where this journal is. Oh, and don't bother lying. We know the truth. We just merely need some...backup information. I've already spoken to your precious daddy." She lifted her hand at Abraham again when he gave no reply, but it was Cameron that answered.

"We don't know!" she yelled. Emily kept her hand in its position but looked to Cameron.

"I don't see that as an answer," Emily replied hatefully.

"The...the...," Cameron sputtered.

"The...the what?" Emily mocked.

Shaven walked over to Emily, but instead of going to her side, he went around her to Cameron. He knelt down and took hold of her legs, pulling them hard to force them straight. Abraham jerked forward at Shaven, but Emily pushed him back. She then lifted her free hand to Cameron's face and pinched it until her lips formed a heart. Cameron let out a groan as her veins pulsed from her face, and then it began to turn color. She began to cough.

"Stop! I'll tell you!" Abraham yelled. "I'll tell you!" Emily's head snapped to him.

"Go on," Shaven said, wrapping Cameron's legs in a chain. She yelled in pain, and this made Emily smile. The chains sizzled against Cameron's skin, giving the air a smell of burning flesh, an aroma that made Emily's smile spread wider across her face.

"Zalvana Peythron *is* our ancestor, and the journal was hers. There is no speculation anymore. Collin told me so, and Jack," Abraham said, defeated, looking over at Cameron. "I didn't tell you because you were safer not knowing the truth."

Emily let go of Cameron's face with a laugh. "It all fits

together now, doesn't it? The journal is the key! We were right, Shaven. Collin was such a fool." She said this while looking at Cameron, who was catching her breath. Emily stood with Shaven at her side, her face turning to stone. Something had dawned on her at that moment. A still sickness formed in her stomach. "When we get my brother back, he'll have a lot of explaining to do," she said. "But, then again, I believe Jack deserves another visit from the both of us, Shaven. Don't you think?"

"I agree."

"Thank you, baby, you were a lot of help," Emily said to Abraham and stood. She kicked Abraham from the side, sending him to the left and slamming against the wall. He laid there motionless. She then left the room with her heels clicking beneath her.

Sawyer

With a groan, he lifted his head but hit something hard. He turned himself to look over, and what he found was the opening underneath his bed. Rubbing his head, he did his best to crawl out from under the bed quietly in case Emily was still there. He listened as he pulled himself up slowly. The room was getting dim, indicating that it was late afternoon. There was no sound until he reached the bedroom door. The sound of the kitchen door opening then closing, and a familiar voice glided up to him. He hurried down the hallway, holding his head in a daze. When he reached the stairs, he found Sander walking towards his room.

"Sander!" Sawyer called. Sander looked up at him, folding a newspaper.

"What's happened to your head? You're bleeding, man!" Sander placed the now folded newspaper into his back pocket to look over Sawyer's injury when he reached him. But Sawyer wasn't in the mood to wait. He would heal slowly, but he would heal. "Wait, wait, I gotta heal it—" Sander began.

"No! We don't have time! Emily was Cameron! Cameron looked like Emily! Emily...somehow she looked just like Cameron. She has Cameron hidden somewhere!"

"Are you sure?"

"I am. I put the pieces together when we were heading here. I knew her story wasn't adding up right. Her face...it switched back and forth to Cameron, then to Emily. Kim was right. We shouldn't have trusted her!"

Sawyer began to rush down the stairs, but Sander quickly took hold of his head and closed his eyes. Sawyer jerked away from him, hurrying to the front door. He knew Sander had healed him by the way he was feeling, but he couldn't stop and say thank you just yet. He had to find Cameron. He had to make her safe. He had to be her Protector this time.

He knew Sander was behind him, and it wouldn't take long for Shane to figure out where they had disappeared to. Slamming the doors behind them, Sawyer sped to Abraham's house. It seemed they had gone to Abraham's house one too many times that same day, but Sawyer just knew something was going on.

Richard

"See you Sunday morning, Helen," Richard said, giving the woman a soft peck on the cheek before she shut the door to her new home. After work, Helen had invited him to dinner, and of course, he couldn't say no. Hesitantly, he turned from the house and moved to his truck. After climbing in, he sat there. Simply sat there, still full from the dinner he had just shared with Helen and her daughter Amy in their new home. The thought of Amy made him think of Cameron and Abraham, and he sighed.

"They've grown up, Jules," he said out loud. "Abraham may not be what I had expected, and I still don't understand where he went, but I'm glad he's back. I just wish you could be here to see him too. To see how beautiful Cameron is. How much of a woman she's grown up to be." He choked back a tear, trying to pull himself together. "I feel like I'm breaking my promise to you. Is it okay to love another when your true love has passed on?" he asked aloud, taking off his glasses and using a hanky from his pocket to clean them. "Look at me…talking to myself." After placing his glasses back on his nose and returning his hanky to his pocket, he rubbed the tip of his nose and pushed down his mustache that he'd let grow out. Letting out a rough cough, he turned the car on and pulled out of Helen's driveway.

He turned up the radio and heard Johnny Cash, one of his favorite singers. He wondered for a moment where Danny was at that time and how he was doing. Since Danny and Kim had left on their honeymoon — which he was still shocked and uncomfortable with — he hadn't heard from either of them. Surely Danny would call his mother soon, so she didn't worry.

Upon reaching his house, he caught sight of a familiar car parked in front of it. He waited a moment before getting out of his car and slowly going over to the parked vehicle. It was hard to see in the car due to the fog that was built up on… the outside? There was no excessive humidity or anything outside to cause it to be fogged. Gently he lifted his hand and wiped the mist from the driver's window, then knocked. No response. He looked into the window closely to find the brown hair of someone facing the other way. A deep fright entered him as he hesitantly opened the door. He lifted his hand to the body and turned the face towards him.

"God!" he shrieked at the sight of Jack, Cameron and Abraham's biological father, whose face was a deep blue, with veins traveling through it.

"Jack? Hello!" He shook the man, but again there was no response. Shaking, he took Jack into his arms and ran into the house with him. He laid Jack on his couch before taking out his cell phone and dialed the first number that came to mind.

Sawyer

"You take the back just in case they try to go out that way, and Sander, you follow me. Be cautious, Shane."

Sawyer went ahead of his pack. Sawyer had known Shane would automatically understand where they were going, and he had met with them the moment they parked. Shane was in his Were form already and ran to the back of the house. Sander had transformed into his Were form as they went towards the house's front door. Because of his late transformation, Sander wasn't able to transform as quickly as the others, so it made sense for him to transform before anything started. Sawyer pushed open the front door and let Sander go in first before following. There was no noise around them except for the simple clacks of their feet on the wooden floors. Sander disappeared into the kitchen as Sawyer looked around the living area for any evidence.

Pound! Crash! Sawyer jumped to his right to only find Shane pushing a shelf back up as he looked at Sawyer apologetically. Shane transformed into his human form again. With rolling eyes, Sawyer went past him and towards the stairs. Sander joined him. They searched many rooms with no luck. All were now in human form.

"What if they really are just not here?" Sander asked.

"They have to be. They wouldn't be anywhere else," Sawyer replied.

"Do you think they could block the room from us?" Shane asked. Sawyer and Sander both gave each other a look.

"What? I can have brilliant ideas too. I mean, they aren't just keeping them in the open. Last time we were here, you looked in the rooms, and there was no one there. Maybe they're hidden from us."

"Nice idea, Shane," Sander complimented.

"It's a good probability, but we still need to keep our guards up," Sawyer replied.

"Sawyer? Sa'yer!"

Sawyer turned to the sudden yell to find Cameron running at him. Sawyer wasn't stupid. He took hold of the girl and threw her against the wall, holding a tight grip around her throat. He looked at the girl, debating whether he should kill her then or torture her for harming his beloved Cameron. The girl tried to speak, but Sawyer only tightened his grip when she tried to do so.

"Sawyer, stop! It's really us!" Abraham dashed out of a room that was down the hall, rubbing his wrists. With a deep build of hurt and shame, Sawyer let go of her, the girl he'd sworn never to harm. Cameron dropped to the ground but was helped up by Shane.

"I'm so sorry, Cameron...I didn't mean to. I was just making sure of...." Sawyer tried to apologize.

"It's...it's fine," Cameron said to him, clinging to Shane before putting a hand out to Sawyer and placing it against his cheek. He lifted his hand and placed it on top of hers. Her hand fell from his cheek as Shane helped her down the hallway. Sawyer watched them till they disappeared down the steps. Abraham slammed his shoulder against Sawyer's as he passed, hurrying to keep up with Cameron. It wasn't until Sander went down the steps behind them that Sawyer moved along.

Everyone met in the large living room except Shane, who searched the house. After Sander healed Abraham and

Cameron's injuries, he helped Abraham put some curtains up over the broken window to keep the cool air out. Sawyer stayed on the other side away from Cameron, ashamed to even share a glance with her. Finally, Shane entered the living room, reassuring them that he had searched the house from top to bottom.

Cameron began. "It wasn't anything I've ever seen before. She literally took my features and made herself into me! It was actually really weird seeing what I looked like in someone else's eyes. Shaven...." She looked over to Abraham, who nodded in return. "He has a power of closing off people's hearing, but it didn't work on me or Abraham. I guess it's because we aren't exactly full-pledged Gathiens, you know? Which by the way, we need to look up more information about us. Since obviously, you know more than you let on," she said to Abraham before looking back at Sander and the group. "If it wasn't for Abraham's gosh damn good thinking, though, we would probably still be tied up in those chains."

"What did they look like? The chains you are speaking of," Sander asked.

"Well, they were gold and very thin like a string. Trust me, don't underestimate them. They stung our skin like it was lava or something, and when he hit me—"

"Shaven beat you with it?" Sawyer said in a growl. Cameron jumped at this, not being able to speak but simply nodded. Sawyer shook his head in anger.

"When he hit me with it, he wore gloves the whole time, so I guess it harms Gathiens too," Cameron said softly.

"Not just Gathiens," Abraham observed. "When Cameron was passed out, they talked about it. It harms anyone in the magical realm, except humans. Humans are the only ones that it does nothing to. They used to use those types of chains in the early 16th century. I remember Collin using them on passing Weres back in the day. I guess they're the same ones he had. They're witch burned."

"Witch burned? There are witches now?" Sander asked.

"The name witch burn doesn't exactly mean witches because they don't exist. It's rare for a Gathien to get a power so strong they can wield an element like earth, water, or fire. The only way to create a chain like that is to wrap it around a Gathien with the power of fire and let it burn with them until they turn into ash on the stage."

"Oh," Sander said with an uneasy expression. He must have regretted asking for he stood, handed Cameron a wrapped white cone, and left the room for a while.

Abraham joined Cameron to look at it. It only took a few seconds for them to look up at each other. "This is a photograph of Collin and Emily!" Cameron said.

"No, it's a painting. You said these chains were created during the 16th Century. If you look at the photo, this painting was made in the 16th century exactly, though Emily was a lot younger," Shane said.

"So this was when Collin got a hold of those chains. It's true," Abraham said in amazement but then looked ill.

"Read it," Sawyer said, annoyed at all the jabber going around. He looked at Abraham and then at Cameron. Their features were so similar, other than their eyes. Abraham's nose crooked at the tip, however, as Cameron's slid down in a perfect C. Both Abraham and Cameron looked down at the newspaper again and began to read it. It was Abraham who looked up first, looking at Cameron then the group.

"You don't think Emily and Shaven are planning to bring Collin back, do you?" Abraham asked.

"We don't think. We know they are. Why else would they ask you about your ancestry? It makes sense, doesn't it?" Sander said when he re-entered, taking a seat close to Sawyer.

"When Emily was talking to Shaven, she said something that really made my stomach turn," Cameron said. Everyone looked at her. "Emily is Collin's sister."

"It makes so much sense now!" Shane shouted before looking to Abraham, who looked ill. "Sorry, man." Before anyone could respond, Cameron continued.

"So you're saying we really are related to this Zalvana Peythron?" Cameron asked.

Abraham looked over at her. "It's true." She looked at him in return.

"How do you know?" Sawyer asked.

"Collin told me. Well, he gave me hints when we were in battle before we killed him." He sighed. "He started with saying he was what made me and you who we are. That his father had mated with our grandmother Zalvana, who was the highest power during that time. She gave birth to a child who was a new kind of being. Part Gathien and part whatever it is we are. Collin's father killed Zalvana when he found out that she wasn't a Gathien but something else. Somehow, when he went to get rid of the child, he or she was gone. Then he said...." He paused, looking at Cameron as if there was something he wasn't sure of saying out loud.

"Go on, Ab. It can't be anything worse than what he told me when I was captured by him," Cameron reassured him.

It took a moment before Abraham continued. "He said 'I may not be a Gathien, and a Were together, but I am the oldest Gathien to be, and now I see that I don't need you to make what I want true.'" He paused, licked his parched lips, and then continued. "'I have Cameron. Our blood will be sacred together. It will be pure. Cameron, who will bow down to me like Zalvana bowed down to my father.'"

Sawyer gritted his teeth, looking down at the floor as Abraham took Cameron's hand when she looked away from him in what seemed like mild shock.

"Collin's father was married to Zalvana, who is your ancestor, and Emily is the sister of Collin. Why else would she try to bring him back? It makes so much sense now. But that would mean...." Sander began but looked over at Shane when he spoke.

"That would make Emily your aunt and Collin, your uncle, wouldn't it?" Shane asked.

"Sadly, yes," Abraham grunted, rubbing his eyes with his palms.

"It may have been okay for people to do incest back then, but these days that is just sick," Shane said.

"I agree," Sawyer said.

Cameron's eyes lifted to Sawyer's as he stared at her.

"Now it's all put together. Emily and Collin were siblings, Collin is dead, and Emily wants revenge," Shane said, quite proud of himself.

"No, she wants to bring him back, and she'll need Zalvana's journal to do it." Sawyer looked at Abraham when he said this. Jack had given Sawyer the journal years before he came to this small town to protect Cameron. After all these years, it had never come to mind that he still had the journal hidden.

A few years prior.

"Sawyer, take this for me," Jack said, handing the book over to him. Sawyer looked at him for a moment and then took the book from him without a question asked. "I need you to hide it. Hide it so no one will find it. Gathiens will come for it, and it's best if they don't get ahold of it. It will keep her safe. I need you to watch after her. You will eventually understand on your own why it's important she is safe. This journal is the key."

Sawyer hadn't known Jack very long, but in only a month's time, he felt as though he had known him all his life. Jack's daughter meant everything to him, Sawyer could tell, but he still didn't know everything about her. All Sawyer knew was that Jack had come to him for help in keeping her safe from the Gathiens. Gathiens had always been enemies to Sawyer's pack, and he knew he had to keep his family and town safe from them at any cost.

"I'll hide it, and I will keep her safe," Sawyer told him and meant it. Jack handed Sawyer a photograph of his daughter. "Where will I find her?" Sawyer asked Jack.

"My daughter's friend...I think he's becoming a Were. He can help you. Here's his address. His name is Daniel. Now, let me explain a woman named Zalvana...."

Present.

"The journal had a spell on it that whoever spoke Zalvana's true full name it would take it back to her wherever she had lost it...Jack told me." He looked to the group for only a moment before looking down. It was all coming back to him now, and silently he continued. "When Zalvana was alive, she had a journal that she wrote her every thought into. This same journal she had a warlock put a spell on so that if she were to ever lose it, her name would be written on it." He spoke under his breath. "Meaning, whoever found her journal would read the name, and it would automatically take the journal, and whoever was holding it back to her at that present time. If Emily wanted Zalvana's journal, she would think it would take her back to Zalvana, and she would kill her before her child is born. It's so simple. I hadn't thought about that journal since Jack gave it to me all those years ago."

Cameron and Abraham's beginning. Placing the pieces together, Sawyer lifted his hand to his chin and glanced about as he thought. He could feel eyes on him but pushed them aside. No one knew that Jack had given him the journal, though it did seem that Abraham knew from the way he stared at Sawyer. He would have to get the journal before Emily could find it. No wonder she had acted as Cameron. She had found Sawyer's room and searched it before she and Shaven left. But where had they gone?

"You knew about me before you even met me? Jack put you up to spy on me?" Cameron's voice said.

"I wasn't spying. I was sent to protect you."

"After all this time, we've been trying to put the pieces together to figure out what we are, and you've had this information the whole time?" Cameron's voice began to rise.

"It was for your protection—"

"—Protection that I don't need any longer and haven't needed for a long time." Her posture tightened, "You could have told us this, and maybe we could have a fighting chance to keep us all safe and get rid of Emily. You and Jack have been lying to me this whole time, haven't you? What else have you lied about?" Everyone sat silently.

"Cameron, you're blowing this out of proportion," Sawyer said calmly, looking to the ground.

"I'm, what?" Cameron shouted as she stood. But Abraham grabbed her wrist, and instead of approaching Sawyer, Cameron walked over to the doorway, looking away from him.

"How did you get out of those chains?" Sander asked out loud.

"Abraham used his strength to push it over his feet," Cameron said without looking to the group.

"Did it leave a scar?" Sander asked. The sound of feet

moving about let Sawyer know that Sander had moved to Abraham's side to look at his hands. It was silent for a moment before Sander spoke again. "It did. Even I cannot completely heal it."

"It's magically bonded, remember?" Abraham said.

"You broke through all of those chains?" Sawyer asked, mostly to himself.

"No. They disappeared once we got to my neck. But that's not important right now. Because apparently, no one here seems to know how to tell the truth. What else don't I know?" Cameron asked, turning to the group then, looking from Abraham to Sawyer.

Sawyer looked up at her, his eyes automatically going to her neck. And there it was—thin but noticeable—a scar crawling across Cameron's neck. He lifted his eyes to hers. "Emily must have set you free. But—" His phone rang. He pulled it out of his pocket and answered. "Hello?"

"Sawyer! He's…he's dying. He's turned blue…he's—"

"Slow down. Breathe. Who's hurt?" Everyone adjusted themselves in their seats to look at Sawyer, who shared a glance with each of them before looking down.

"Jack! I found him in his car in front of my house. I think he's dying; what do I do?"

"Richard, I need you to listen to me very closely." Cameron went to him and got close enough to him to listen to the phone call. "Lay him on his side, and I need you to place a hot rag on his forehead. Then, I need you to do something very important for me, all right?" *Emily knew where the journal was*, he thought frantically.

"All right." He heard a rustling over the phone…a door opened and then shut. There was movement again, and then the phone was picked up once more.

"Now, go into Cameron's old bedroom." He waited until

he heard Cameron's door being opened on the other end of the line. "Underneath her bed should be a box that she has her paintings in. Pull it out from under the bed and push it aside." He waited until he was satisfied. "Feel her flooring. There should be one floor panel that is slightly lifted on the edge...pull that up and pull out the box that is inside of it." He heard Richard set the phone down so he could pull the box out, and then he picked up the phone again.

"I have it," Richard said.

"Keep that on your person, and do not let it out of your sight."

Sawyer hung up his phone. Emily had been at Richards... she had followed Jack, and now she knew where Richard lived. She'd done something to Jack, probably to get information from him; that or to torture Cameron and Abraham some more. "Richard said he found Jack in his car, and he was turning blue. Does this mean anything to you?" he asked, mostly to Cameron, but it was Abraham who answered.

"Emily can kill with just a touch...she can suck the life out of you."

"Shane, Sander, and Abraham, come with me. Cameron, you stay here," Sawyer said.

"You hid it under my bed," Cameron shook her head as her mouth turned into a straight line, "You've lied to me this entire time! You knew about the journal, and you didn't come to help me because you wanted to. You did it out of a bribe! I don't need your help, Sawyer. I can help Jack on my own," Cameron protested.

Sawyer looked at her and sighed. "I know you can, but I'd feel much better if you stayed here until I call. Richard will be bringing Jack here soon, and I need you here to help him."

"Stop treating me like I'm helpless, and you're not going to keep anything else from me. I'm going. I don't trust your judgment." In a flash, she disappeared.

Her words sent knives into his heart. He had never meant to hurt her by keeping this from her. To be completely honest, he hadn't thought of the journal since he'd hidden it inside Cameron's room all those years ago.

"Let's go, guys," Sawyer said.

CHAPTER 7

Emily

She peeked from the closet, watching the man as he crawled underneath the bed, phone in hand. She couldn't hear who was on the other end of the line, but she did see the man pull a small box out from underneath the bed. A large smile filled her face when she saw the box.

When the phone was hung up, she silently followed the man through the house. She watched as the man took a bag and began to fill it with things, things that she had no use for. Her eyes traveled over to where Jack was laying. This time she grinned, proud of her work. It was time for her to call Shaven.

At that moment, she closed her eyes and blew softly into the air. The soft screech echoed into the air, and it didn't take long for Shaven to appear. She could see him through the window to the front lawn. The man zipped up his bag, went to Jack, and picked him up by his arms. He began to go out the front door, dragging Jack with him, but Emily had no time to spare. Shaven took hold of Jack's body and tossed it aside. The man fell forward as Emily sped to get in front of him.

"Hello," she said to him. In a split second, she lifted her

hands, took hold of the man's head, and jerked it to the right, almost fully around. The man's body fell to the ground.

"No!" A scream came from Emily's left. She jumped in surprise but quickly took the bag from the limp body and pulled the journal out of the bag. Her laugh echoed in an evil trance. Cameron came out of the woods shrieking. Emily waved the journal mockingly. Finally, she had succeeded.

"Oh, don't worry about that, Cameron," Emily said, nudging the body. "He didn't have long to live anyways. He would have had to grow old while you stay young looking. That would be quite a burden." Cameron's head shook from side to side before she lifted her hands. Emily's smile went stern in an instant. Her teeth gritted, and she placed the journal in her jacket pocket. "Let's not be hasty, *pumpkin*."

Cameron

My feet hit the ground, and I stepped from the light. How could Sawyer lie to me? After all this time, he had so many chances to tell me the truth. Jack had Sawyer watch over me, and Sawyer had the journal this whole time? And Abraham knew about Zalvana too and never said a thing! What else had they lied to me about?

It didn't matter right now...Richard and Jack needed my help. I knew after hearing Richard on the phone something bad was about to go down, but I didn't expect what I saw. The moment I walked out of the woods, I saw Emily's hands placed firmly on the sides of Richard's head, and before I could move, his face was forced to the side, and his body fell to the ground lifelessly. Anger, grief, nervousness, and every other emotion you could think of filled me. I lifted my hands at her, ready to blow her up. Her words didn't hurt me now. "Cameron, no!" Abraham's voice came from behind me. I stood my ground, not even giving him a glance.

"I don't need a lecture right now, Ab. I need support, dammit!" I said. I hadn't meant for it to come out so hatefully, but I guess with every emotion jerking through me, I didn't want the aggravation. It was either he helped me, or I did it all on my own. "Now, let's take her," I said. Abraham ran past me towards Emily. It was a stupid move, I had to admit. But it was a surprise to me that Abraham wasn't running after Emily. He was going after Shane, who was trying to be a badass and take Emily on his own. Abraham threw himself at Shane, throwing them both to the ground. Emily's laugh still echoed.

"Come on, you mongrels; is that all you've got?" Emily yelled.

"Who are you calling a mongrel?" I said and finally let my flame out. Emily's hands lifted a second before the light was to touch her and blocked it. It felt as if it had happened in slow motion. Emily's hands pushed the light in another direction, and my eyes flickered to the direction it was heading. My feet seemed to be going slowly, but in reality, I was running faster than I ever had. My eyes went back and forth from the flame to the direction I was running. To the person I was running to. "Abraham!" I yelled. Even then, my voice seemed to go slowly. Abraham turned to me. I knew before I got to him that I wasn't going to be fast enough. A loud yell of agony filled my ears, but it wasn't Abraham's. It was my own.

The bright light filled the whole ground. My arms went around Abraham's body as it fell, and I fell with it. I screamed in sadness and fright. My body shook with adrenalin. I could hear the pounding fight on the other side of me as Sawyer and Sander fought Emily. Shane was next to me, but I gave him no glance. As I held onto Abraham, I closed my eyes. Our pulses mimicked each other's. "Send me your strength, Abraham," I spoke to him. I didn't move when I felt his strength fill me...I just opened my eyes and continued to hold him. Finally, I turned my free hand towards Emily, who had the journal folded out. I knew what she was about to say when her mouth fell open, so I released my light again. Like we were a whole, I saw through Emily's force field. Emily thought of Zalvana's name before she spoke. "Zalvana Peythron!" I said with her.

Still connected with Abraham, we were pulled from the ground and thrown back down like a basketball being beaten against the ground. Richard's house was no longer in our view. Sawyer, Sander, and Shane were nowhere to be seen. The air was warm, and beneath us was grass. Fields of grass and woods surrounded us.

I looked down at Abraham, who lay there motionless, and before I knew it, I heard shouts and the sound of horses coming towards us from down the field we had landed in. An arrow flew past my torso and into a tree trunk behind me, and it was then I knew I needed to get myself and Abraham out of there. I still had no idea where we were or where Emily was, but I knew these guys didn't look like they were coming to help us. I rose, putting my hands up in front of me, and thought only of the men holding flowers. Nothing happened. They continued to get closer. "What the...?" I said to myself, looking at my hands that barely sparked.

"Come with me!" I looked to my left to find a young female signaling for us to follow. I pointed to Abraham and began to pull him. She joined my side and picked up his feet with one hand and lifted her other hand towards the men, then squinted her eyes. I looked at the men after she did this to find their hats had turned into squids. She placed Abraham's feet on the ground to push open a door. I would have never guessed it was home since the door was connected to a large boulder. Without question, I entered, laying Abraham on a nearby rug. I turned back to look at the girl. Her hair was black, but with every move she made, you could see a flash of burgundy highlights. "You are an insane one, you are," she said to me, placing a rag on Abraham's head. It wasn't until then that I noticed her clothing was weird. It was a dress but tied in the back. When she turned to me again, I could see her face was a little dirty, and she wore no makeup.

"Where are we?" I asked her. She went past me to get a bottle that laid on a placemat on the floor. As she opened it, a fizz of green escaped it, then she went past me again and tilted Abraham's head back. "Whoa! Hold up! What are you doing?" I asked, rushing to Abraham's side.

"Do you want him to live or not?" she asked me. I hesitated before backing away. She tilted Abraham's head until his mouth fell open. She poured the liquid into Abraham's mouth then laid him down. "Now," she said, wiping her hands on her dress. "I do not know what town you are from, but obviously, you are not aware of the boundaries."

"Boundaries?" I asked.

"Precisely. There are many things happening around here, and you do not want to be caught in the middle of them." She stopped to eye me. "Your name?" Something inside me told me I wasn't supposed to tell her the truth about our identities just yet. So quickly, I blurted the first thing that came to mind.

"Anne. Anne…Burgundy. Anne Burgundy."

"I do not believe I have met any Burgundys in this town. Well, wherever you are from, you have no use for fashion either," she said. I looked down at myself. I thought I looked rather cute. Besides, from what she was wearing, you would think she was a peasant from the 16th century or something. Wait….

"What year is it?" I asked her. She looked at me sternly but answered anyway.

"It is August 4, 1533. Do you not know this?"

"Do you know...." I stopped for a moment to relax. "Zalvana Peythron?"

"Why, I certainly do. I am her sister, Cintia Peythron. You just missed her. What do you have to do with her?" Cintia asked.

I smiled. Cintia still watched me closely, but I didn't care. She was my great aunt? I wanted to just hug her, but, yeah, that would have been very weird. "Wait a moment." Cintia left the room, but in only a moment, returned with a folded gown in hand. She let it unfold in the air as she cleaned it off. "You cannot go around dressed like that. People will think something. While you are changing, I expect you will tell me why you were out in the open like that and why your friend here was at the edge of death." I didn't like it when she said that. I didn't ever want to think about Abraham dying. I had gone through way too much to lose him now. "You will also tell me why your light did not work." She was very forward and too trusting.

I didn't know what to say to her when she spoke of my powers. I knew that she was gifted too, from when I saw her make squids appear on the men's heads. But how did she know I was gifted too? "You'll also tell me why your light didn't work"...she'd seen me when I tried to turn those men's guns into flowers. She had the same powers Abraham and I did.

I followed Cintia as she led me to a small room. There was a fairly large mirror next to a small bed, and that was it other than a small wooden box that sat in the corner, which I assumed held her clothes. "Go on," she waved to me. I hesitated before undressing myself as Cintia placed sheets on the bed. It was so awkward dressing in front of her. It reminded me of when I'd first appeared at Sawyer's house a year ago, and Kim had helped me into my pajamas. Little did I know that that night would be the start of all of this. Even though Cintia didn't look at me, I still felt like I was naked. I kept my bra and underwear on so that I didn't have to worry about her seeing my you-know-what's. "Your undergarments are strange," Cintia said with her back turned to me still. "Now explain to me where you are from. How did you get here?"

"We didn't know where we were. We just sorta...," I glanced up at her backside, "Sorta appeared."

"Have you been playing with magic? A girl like you needn't be messing with a Gathien's scorn," Cintia said, still turned from me, "Your friend —"

"Brother. He's my brother."

Cintia turned to me then. I didn't know if it was because I'd said he was my brother or because I couldn't seem to be able to tie my own gown, but her face twisted into an uncomfortable look. I looked away from her to continue tying my gown, which was actually pretty and fit me well. But there were so many ties going down the back I could hardly reach half of them. My arms weren't that freaking long. I didn't complain, though. At least I wasn't being forced to wear something like what Cintia wore. It was a bit selfish of me, but the one she gave me was a lot prettier. It was a light blue gown that went past my ankles, with strands of sparkles going down the sides and a vintage design that went over the center of my chest that was entwined with very small pearls. "Look up at me, dear," she said to me, placing a hand under my chin. I looked into her eyes for a split second before looking away. Her hand fell from my face and to her side after only a second, and then she backed away from me like I was some kind of ghost. "What did you say your name was again?"

"Anne." What was my last name? Brown? No. Burgers?

"Your last name?"

"B...burrrger...Burgundy!"

She exited the room. My heart was beating so fast I almost wanted to puke. I walked over to a near mirror that was just as tall as my body so I could look at myself. I turned around to look at my back and did my best to tie the strings as tight as I could so that they wouldn't come apart. I turned again at the sound of a knock to find Abraham standing there. His left arm was pulled up into a cloth-like sling, and the left part of his face was bruised. I didn't wait for a second to go to him. I hugged him tightly, and with his free hand, he hugged me back. We didn't say anything. I went back over to the mirror to check on my strings that I had tied somewhat before turning back to Abraham and exiting the room.

When we got to the living room, I noticed some new things. It wasn't very big, and the walls seemed as if they would fall down any moment. It also, from what I could see, only had two rooms, the living room and a very small kitchen. If you'd even call it a kitchen because it was nothing like our time. *That's our aunt,* I said silently to Abraham. But he hadn't seemed to have heard me at all. "Ab?"

"Yes?" Abraham replied.

"Did you hear me?" I asked.

"I hear you fine. It's my arm that's messed up, not my hearing."

"No! Did you hear my...," I looked around to see if anyone was in hearing range before whispering, "Call? I told you something, but you didn't seem to hear me."

"That's because I didn't hear you. We won't have what we had in our time, Cam, because technically we don't exist."

Cintia came into the room with a tray of crackers and vegetables and laid it on a wooden table in front of us.

"Why did you help us?" Abraham asked her.

"With hard times like this, those that share the same light as me are worth saving."

CHAPTER 8

Cameron

There was a soft click on the other side of the room. Abraham and I both turned towards the rock door. My stomach dropped at the sight of the door coming open. I thought those men had found out about us for sure. My hand reached Abraham's free arm and grasped it firmly. Cintia rushed from a room across from the one I had been in and welcomed the man who entered, and I let out a breath.

The man entered, letting Cintia take off his coat. He was tall and muscular with curly, neatly cut hair. I couldn't see his face well, but from what I could see, he had a beard that was shaved lightly and curved around his chin so that it left a part unshaven in the middle. He also had a mustache, but it wasn't like Richard's. It was more of a shaved mustache but curled so that it flowed to his cheekbones. Also, his shirt was cut down the middle to his belly button and sagged on his arms.

"Look at this!" The man shouted to Cintia, who took the envelope from him. I leaned in to see what was written on it, but Cintia was too quick. She took the envelope over to the wooden table and sat down to look at the letter.

"'To those it may concern, you have been cordially

invited to attend the Spring Ball that will be held at the Du Gant residence—" Cintia began to read but was interrupted by the man, who yelled once again excitedly.

"The Du Gant residence! To the governor's ball!"

"'On the fifth night of August,'" Cintia continued.

"Tomorrow, and I've only just received it! Can you believe it, C? We are to go to the ball!"

"Come now, Derek; we have no business going to a fancy ball like that."

"Oh, but you have yet to hear the best part! Zalvana was invited to the ball as well. Specifically invited to a private encounter with Gaspard! Do you know what this means?"

"This means we are in a big dip of trouble. That is what it means! You bad thing. How could you let her go? She will let that horrid man see her light, and then it will be the end of us all! Besides, what would people think if I was on your arm?"

"No, no, no. We talked about it, Zal and I before she headed out to your father's farm. We have a plan, and the thoughts of others is not important."

"Gaspard is the name of Collin's father. I know what time we have come back to." Abraham whispered so that only I could hear.

"How rude of me...shush now, Derek."

My mouth was flat open, and with embarrassment, I closed it. My tongue was so dry. Gaspard was Collin's dad? It was all starting to make sense! The journal had come back to this time because this was the year Zalvana was killed. The last time she would have had the journal in her possession.

Cintia turned her eyes towards me and Abraham, signaling for the man to go quiet. His eyes turned to us too. "These are my guests, Ms. Anne Burgundy and her brother...." She continued to stare at Abraham for him to answer. Abraham looked down at me for a moment before the shine of understanding lit his eyes. He looked back at Cintia.

"My name is Jack," Abraham said. With all the excitement, I had forgotten about everything that had happened at home. Was Jack even all right? Anger filled my bones at the thought of his lies until I remembered…Richard was dead. Tears filled my eyes instantly. I knew Sawyer, Shane, and Sander had to be fine. I couldn't believe that Sawyer had lied to me. I thought all of this time that we were one and true to each other. How could he do that to me? How could my own father even do that to me? What about Shaven? Had he arrived at Emily's aid and come here too? Or had he continued to fight Sawyer and his pack? Still, deep down, I was angry with Sawyer, and Abraham too. Had they spoken up in the first place, we would have probably had this Emily situation resolved. Emily had to be stopped, or all of this would have been for nothing. Richard would have died for nothing.

Abraham saw my eyes tearing up and pinched my hand as hard as he could with his free hand. It surely didn't make me stop crying, but it did take my mind off the past…or future. I didn't even know.

"Well, hello there, Jack. And fancy meeting you, Miss Anne. I don't believe we have met any Burgundys, have we, Cintia?" the man asked, placing a hand out to Abraham, who took it in a firm shake.

"No, sir, we haven't."

"You have been invited to the ball too, no doubt?" he asked Abraham.

"I don't believe so, Derek, because they have only just arrived in town," Cintia answered.

"Ah! Well, they should be invited, should they not? Instead of you and I attending together, Ms. Anne can accompany me, and Sir Jack can accompany you."

"Yes, sir."

It was obvious that Derek was considered to be above Cintia's station by the way she spoke to him. She didn't look very happy at the thought of going to the ball, but I figured she couldn't tell him no. She took Abraham by his good arm and took him to the same backroom I had been in before.

I jumped a little when I looked back at Derek, who had been staring at me. He had moved closer to me and was so close I could see the color of his eyes. Sky blue. He almost reminded me of Prince Erik from *The Little Mermaid*. "You look familiar to me. Have we met before?" he asked me.

"I don't think so. But it's good to meet you." I didn't understand why he looked at me weirdly until it hit me. I wasn't talking like they did way back when. They were more proper and didn't do the things we did in the 2000s. Maybe I could try to lighten it up a bit? I mean, I'd seen a lot of old-time movies, and wasn't *The Other Boleyn Girl* based on this time or something like that? "We just got out of some trouble with some guards. Cintia helped us."

"The bandits, I suppose. They have been hunting down O'ahee people for weeks! Now that Gaspard is governor, he has put out a sum of money for their heads."

"O'ahee people?" I asked.

"Now, Derek, are you in here scaring our guests?" Cintia asked when she and Abraham reentered. Abraham was dressed in an odd outfit...a gray overcoat with a tucked-in white shirt underneath. It was kinda moth-eaten, too.

"Not at all! I was simply explaining how the bandits have been out trying to capture O'ahee people—"

There was a loud bang from the back of the home. Cintia ran to it with Derek right behind her, and then Abraham and I followed. In the back room, the walls were wooden. The best way to describe them was to say they looked like the inside of a tree trunk. A couple more thumps were made until Cintia pushed open a small square door. It opened to the outside, letting the bright sunshine in. The orange glow indicated that the sun was going down.

A huge bird flew in, and Cintia lifted her arm to let it rest there, but its claws did nothing to her skin. The bird was beautiful, though. Its tail was as long as my arm, pale white with strings of gold, while its eyes were as big as an owl's and were a golden hue. Eyelashes as long as my pinky flushed from its eyes too, and its mouth was perfectly pointed. The feathers on its neck were even beautiful in their own way, curved over each other in a yellow pattern. The rest of its body was pure white...even its feet.

"This is Edenaun, my guardian," Cintia said proudly. She looked over at me at the same time Edenaun did, as if she were studying me.

"Your guardian?" Abraham asked from behind me. Derek went over to the bird and began to pet its spine until its eyes turned to him, then he began to softly stroke its head. Cintia was eying Abraham as Derek let Edenaun on his arm.

"Edenaun is a cucuio...a light guardian for O'ahee people. Every O'ahee person has one. Well, except for me. I'm merely a human," Derek said with a choked laugh. Someone normal! It was about time. "They are strange birds with good hearts. They help those who cannot see without the light. Eden here helps me all the time. They are so fascinating."

If the cucuio bird was a guardian to O'ahee people, and Cintia was one, then shouldn't that make me and Abraham one too? I'd never seen a bird like that or had one help me in the dark. I could have used one during the time of Collin's battle.

"They are very rare during this time. You should know this. You may be strangers to these parts, but I know what I saw," Cintia said.

Abraham and I glanced at each other before Abraham spoke again. "I don't believe I know what you're talking about, ma'am," Abraham said.

"You may not, for you were nearly dead at the scene; however, you, my dear, should know." She looked at me. I looked up at Abraham, who looked at me before looking to the floor. *Do I need to tell her what I am?* The way she looked at me, I knew she had a good idea already. But how did I tell her what I was when even I didn't know? I rubbed my arm as the nerves rose in me. I began to feel sick to my stomach.

I decided I might as well go ahead and tell her. She was my blood, after all.

"Honestly? I don't know what we are. Where we're from is much different than now. Um...." I looked around the wooden room for anything to call to me, but there wasn't anything small enough for me to catch. "Can I just show you?" I asked.

A smile crossed Cintia's lips. "We are waiting."

"Okay." I thought about it for a moment before closing my eyes. I thought only of being placed outside the door. I continued to think of this, but I didn't feel any warmth come to me. My eyes came open to see if anything had happened, but I was still in front of everyone, just standing there like an idiot. "Nothing happened," I said, looking at Abraham, whose eyebrows had squinted in thought.

"Try pushing me down," Abraham said. I rose my palms towards him and closed my eyes once again. I thought of pushing him down with my light...forcefully to the ground. I peeked one eye open to look at my palms. Only a mere spark came from them. Cintia must have seen this, for she gasped. I opened both of my eyes then to look at her. Her hands had gone to her mouth before she let them fall.

"I believed it to be so! You have the power of light, do you not?" she asked me. I nodded.

"We do. We thought it best to keep it secret until we saw you were someone we could trust. We've been forced here from another realm. We know no one here," Abraham said calmly. He was lying to them! I looked at Cintia with disbelief. Obviously, she found this odd and came to my side. I guess they had seen weirder things because neither Cintia nor Derek questioned us about being from another realm.

"Any O'ahee people are welcome here. Though it does explain your odd use of language," Derek said.

"Thank you. We just aren't that educated for this time, and being here makes it all even more confusing. Last time I checked, we were human beings," I added, looking up at Abraham, who rolled his eyes.

"We were never human, Cam." Before Abraham could stop himself, his face flushed. My eyes widened.

"Cam?" Derek asked, looking at me.

"My middle name is Cameron. Sometimes I get called Cam. What exactly are we?" I asked as quickly as I could so that he didn't ask any more questions. It worked. Derek let it slide, and so did Cintia, who continued the conversation with Abraham.

"Not O'ay-hee. It's O-ah-ee. We are magical beings from the old time. Some say the heavens bless us."

"Magic? So you're saying there's more than just us out there. Like...," I glanced over at Abraham again before looking back at Cintia, "Like Gathiens and werewolves."

"Many creatures live in these ages. The ones that live now may not...they may not exist where you are from."

"What kind of creatures, exactly?" I asked.

"Let me see. Warlocks, brownies, berameds, visible ghosts, protectors...." Derek named them off.

"You mean all of those exist? What's a brownie?" I asked,

keeping myself from laughing.

"Brownies are spirits that help humans and keep them safe. Though if you cross them, they can take or even destroy anything they please. Humans normally can't see them, and when they do, the brownie disappears and never comes back," Cintia explained.

"They disappear? Like they die?" I asked.

"Yes. They turn into dust." How sad.

"Protectors...." I thought of Gavin automatically. My heart seemed to skip a beat when I did. I hadn't seen him in such a long time, and I wondered if he'd changed...if he was safe. I hoped deep down that he was called to Sawyer's aid after we were pulled here. They would need as much backup as they could get with Shaven still there and with so many questions unanswered. "I thought a protector's gift was just something you got when you turned into a Were?"

"Oh, no, dear. Protectors have been around longer than O'ahee people. Though only Weres can become one, it isn't given out freely. It's not something you should wish to become."

"Can you tell us why we are—how we are?" Abraham asked.

"No one really knows when or how we came to be. Though, I fear, tomorrow may become the end of our generation." Cintia sighed at this. Did she not realize everything we'd said to her? Obviously, nothing bad happened, because hello...I was still here, and so was Abraham. I looked at Cintia for the longest time, trying to see if I looked anything like her. She was a thin woman, tall, and had a lot of freckles, but she was darker than me and didn't have light hair like I did.

"What do you mean?" Abraham asked. His voice had changed to a more serious tone.

"My sister, Zalvana, is doing something that no one else

was brave enough to do." She came closer to us and lowered her voice, even though there was no one else to hear her. "She's giving herself up to Gaspard. He's the governor of our lands and is also a Gathien. You would be surprised to know that Gathiens aren't our worst enemies. Weres are a much more challenging enemy. But, they will help us maintain a high balance and agree with the absurd ways of Gathien's. If Zalvana was to be with a Gathien, I don't think things would be the same for us. See, Zalvana plans to convince Gaspard that she isn't an O'ahee creature, and she intends to have a child with him." Cintia said this looking at me and then to Derek.

"How are Were's our worst enemies?" I asked, a bit offended by her words. Abraham elbowed me in the side. I glared up at him then looked back to Cintia. Cintia pushed my question aside as she opened up the wooden window.

"I must get ready to go; go on now," Derek said as Eden flew out the window. Cintia closed it once Eden was out of sight. Derek and Cintia left the room, leaving Abraham and I alone. Abraham's face hadn't changed since Cintia brought up Zalvana and Gaspard.

"We can't go to this ball, Ab. I know for sure Emily will be there."

"I'm thinking." He was silent for a moment. "I think we have to go, Cam, because of the very reason Emily will be there. I know what she's up to. She's put it into her head that if she kills Zalvana before she gives birth, she'll end our whole line...which may be true. If she gets rid of Zalvana, we would have never been born, and so Collin would have never been defeated. We have to go and make sure she gets nowhere near Zalvana."

"Come along," Cintia said behind us. I looked to her and Abraham as well. She lifted her hand to us and waved for us to follow her. She wore a blanket-like coat over her shoulders that was tied around her neck. Derek was nowhere to be seen. "We will be staying at Derek's tonight. Unless you have somewhere else to go?"

"Oh no, that would be wonderful," I replied.

"Good. My home is not quite big enough for such accommodations, as you have seen. Derek is waiting outside for us in his buggy." Abraham left the room as I waited behind for Cintia, who was quickly cleaning the room. I watched her silently until she turned to me.

"Thank you," I said to her.

"Think nothing of it," she replied with a smile. "Come." She took my arm, and we both left the home and went out to find Derek petting the face of a horse that was connected to a wagon. The horse was huge, with feet the size of my forearm and a tail as long as my whole body. Its hair was long, and the tail was pulled up into a braid so that it didn't drag on the ground. It was magnificent. Abraham was sitting in the back, speaking with Derek as Cintia and I climbed onto the wagon. The horse was breathing deeply ahead of us.

"I hope you do not mind, but the ride will be rather bumpy," Derek said, turning from us.

He swung the rope he held, and the horse began to move its feet. We travelled deeper into the woods until we came to a dirt road. As we traveled, Abraham and Derek continued a conversation that I didn't really listen to as I looked to Cintia.

"What happened between us and the Gathiens?" I asked.

She was silent for a moment as if to consider her answer before finally pulling the blanket from her shoulders and laying it on her lap. "Gathiens have always been jealous, ignorant, and the utmost of greedy creatures. For centuries we lived in peace until Unwin, Gaspard's grandfather, became governor of our land. He was a mad man and always held a grudge against us for being as powerful as, or perhaps more powerful than, them. He always yearned for more power and was the first to ever wield the power of earth. None had heard of such a power until he became of age. You see, Gathien's only get their powers when they reach the age of puberty. His hatred of other magical beings became a strong desire to destroy us. He never wanted others to overcome his power, even at a young age. Kazamar, Gaspard's father, was the worst. Taught by his father, he became one of the most powerful Gathiens and the most wicked. O'ahee people had to go into hiding because of the beheadings. Even werewolves went to their own lands so as to stay out of Gaspard's reach. The Du Gant line continues to cause turmoil. By and by, we have had to keep to ourselves, and I would not be here had it not been for Derek's kind ways." She looked over at Derek. "He's the second hand to the governor, and had it not been for him, I would have been taken captive with the others that once lived in my village. But don't you worry, he's on our side and would never hand us over." She smiled up at Derek's back. "He is in charge of the humans, and Gregory, the third hand, is in charge of the werewolves. Here we are." Finally, a stone castle came into view. Upon arriving, a couple of women came out of the home to greet us. It was dark now, and they carried candles.

"Cintia, dear, you've been gone for days! Did Derek tell you the good news?" a blonde woman called. When the wagon came to a stop, Derek was the first to get down and helped us get out of the wagon. Abraham was at my side as we followed them into the home.

"Good is not what I would say," Cintia said as Derek chuckled beside her. The women were ahead of us, chatting.

"Did you hear what Cintia said about the Gathiens?" I asked Abraham.

"I did. All of this hatred because of jealousy," Abraham replied.

"Qwyen will escort you to your room, Jack, and Georgiana will take you, Anne. I hope you find your accommodations fitting, and we will see you on the morrow," Derek said to us. The blonde from before led Abraham away, and the other took off, leading me to a room far up the stairs.

"Thank you," I told the woman as she opened the door to my room. After she shut it behind me, I looked about. There was a small, round cot in the corner of the room, but it was long enough for my body to rest on it. I didn't change before I lay down on it. The ground was cold and musty, and I knew then it was going to be a long night.

The next day.

It was an even longer morning, I felt. I had been woken up for breakfast at the crack of dawn by Georgiana...if you would call it breakfast, that was. We were given eggs, bread, and some meat that I could swear was in the shape of a beaver. Abraham joined me around one, dressed in a nice jacket that was black with fur on the shoulders and a baggy white shirt underneath with tights. It was a hilarious sight. He also wore a hat with a feather that dangled on one side.

"Dashing," I said to him, laughing.

"Wait until you see what you'll be wearing," he said to me, which shut me up. Cintia came into the room then.

"Follow me, Anne."

I went with her down the hall to a back room. There were a few gowns laid out, but one was hanging across the room next to the window. It was draped in a silky green cloth, had sleeves that dangled at the wrists, and an inner gown that was tan. "Derek brought us some gowns to choose from. I will be wearing the blue across the way, and you will wear the green. I believe it to not cause much attention to you. Gaspard is to believe that myself and Zalvana are not O'ahee, so you must not act as one either. Georgiana will help you with your gown. I will see you soon."

And with that, she left the room. Georgiana joined me only a second later and helped me into my gown. She was already dressed in a nice yellow dress.

When she was pulling my gown over my shoulders, she caught sight of my necklace. "That's a beautiful piece," she said to me. I looked down at it and took it in my hand. It was small yet warm to my touch. I had almost forgotten I was wearing it. Sawyer must be worried, and I was worried for him in return. I may not agree with his decisions, but I wanted him to be all right.

After she was done braiding my hair, she pulled it up into a bun on my head and tied it with a tan bow. There was a knock at the door, and Cintia came in. Her dress was beautiful...dark blue with a grey underlining. It hugged her body until it reached her rear, where it expanded out down to her feet. Her hair was down, and wavy, and only a few inches were pulled back with a ribbon. "Are we ready?" she asked. "The ball is about to begin."

"We are," Georgiana said, smiling at me through the mirror.

"Get on with it then." With that said, Georgiana and I exited the room to join Cintia, Qwyen, Abraham, and Derek, who were waiting for us. We left the home and followed Derek, who led us to the front of the home. I looked in awe at the carriage that was awaiting us. I'd never been in a carriage. It was nothing like the wagon we had traveled in the night before.

Derek opened the door, took my hand, and helped me

into the carriage. I smiled at him as he did so. After I sat
down, Abraham crawled in behind me, taking a seat next to
me. Derek did not get in, but Cintia came in after us, followed
by the other women. "Where's Derek?" I asked Cintia.

"He will be leading the horses," Cintia replied, crossing
her arms the opposite of how anyone else would cross their
arms...her left arm over the other. My eyes looked up at
Cintia, down at her arms, over at Abraham's arms that were
placed on his knees, and then down at my own. Cintia and
I were sitting the exact same way. Quickly I put my arms
down, crossing my fingers together, and then looked out the
very small window. Everything was so different. Where I
lived, there was some free land that wasn't built on just yet,
but we lived very close to the town. Here there was hardly
any city except a couple of homes we passed. That was until
we came up to a downward hill that led to a very old looking
city. It reminded me of the movie *Hunchback of Notre Dame*,
the Disney version. But then again, it seemed more....

"Welcome to Ventral," Cintia said, looking at me now. I
glanced over at Abraham, who was looking down at his hands
in thought. "Now, you two, there is something I need to tell
you before you are fed to the dogs. Figuratively speaking, of
course," Cintia started as she straightened herself, cleared
her throat, and then continued. "Gaspard and his son Collin
are completely and unutterably against O'ahee creatures like
ourselves. So it would be best, you see, to keep your mouths
shut while in the city walls. Keep your light to yourself, unless
you would like to lose your heads." With that said, Cintia
looked back out the window.

I would have laughed had she not seemed so serious
about our heads. I looked out the window too, and when I did,
I found that we were in the city limits now. It was completely
different than it looked from far away. Every building looked

newly built, yet the people who walked by told another story. Some people we passed were really dirty, as others wore the fanciest clothes I'd ever seen!

The clicking of the horse's feet distracted me for a moment, and when I looked back up, I saw something that nearly made me jump out of my seat. A woman appeared right next to the carriage levitating with it as it moved. Her eyes were pitch black, and her hair was as white as a piece of paper. "Shoo!" I turned to find Cintia swatting at the creature, who did exactly that. "Goblin in disguise," Cintia said, shutting the curtains. "I expect they weren't invited to the ball."

"Actually, Tomas was invited as a Chester! Can you believe that?" Derek said overhead. Cintia covered a smile.

"Tomas is not a goblin; he is only joking," Cintia said to us before putting her head out the window and calling to Derek. "Though sometimes I would say he could have been a frog at some point!" Derek laughed.

Once we reached the Du Gant residence, Derek hopped off the carriage, tied the horses to a nearby post, and then opened the door to help us out. Abraham was the last to step out, and he closed the carriage door behind him. "My arm, milady." I turned to Derek, who had his arm held out to me. Abraham did the same with Cintia, and they walked behind us as we traveled up the stairs. Once we reached the top of the steps — that I could have sworn were never going to end — Derek whispered our names to a very short man, who turned to the crowd down below. He yelled our names before giving a very hard pound on the ground with his… stick thing. After we took a few steps, Cintia and Abraham's names were called the same way ours had been. The music that played was slow, but it was pretty. "The male in the dark green overcoat is Collin. Stay close to my side, m'dear." The hairs on the back of my neck rose at his name. I straightened myself before looking to my right.

And there he was. The nasty git Collin, who'd ruined my life, looked exactly the same. I figured after all those years, he would have changed at least a bit. But with the exceptions of his odd clothing, longer hair, and that he wasn't trying to murder someone...yet...he seemed the same.

"Ab," I whispered, turning to see if he was behind me, and to my relief, he was. Abraham squeezed through the crowd, no longer arm in arm with Cintia, who was nowhere to be seen. "Where's Cintia?" I asked, with my arm still tightly tangled with Derek's. Abraham's face had gone pale. Paler than usual, at least.

"She went to find Zalvana." Zalvana, the woman who'd started it all. My great grandmother. It would be a lie to say I wasn't really excited to see what she looked like. I looked a lot like my mom, and when I was growing up, everyone said I looked like her except for my attitude...that was like my dad. I wondered if Mom looked anything like Zalvana. Cintia had black hair with a shine of burgundy, but my mom and I shared a light brown. So it would only make sense if Zalvana had that color of hair, right? Or maybe it had faded in our ancestry, and Mom got it from her grandparents or whatever. I didn't know. It would be cool to see, even though it would be bad if she saw us and totally freaked if I did look like her.

I looked up at Ab for only a moment to see that he was gazing out to the crowd, then I looked over at Derek. I was just about to say something when there was a loud crash. I turned around to find a brunette male staggering to stand up. Another male was pointing at him and yelling while he pulled out a whip with his other hand. When he lifted it into the air, something in me just popped.

I knew exactly how it felt to be whipped with a whip like he was holding. It hurt more than anything I could even describe! And maybe it was my superhero senses kicking in, but I didn't want that poor boy to be whipped. I wouldn't want anyone to go through that. Before I knew it, I was pushing through the crowd.

"Wait! No!" I yelled. I kept tripping over my gown but did my best to not fall down. That would have been a freaking funny sight...me falling down in the middle of a bizarre scene like that. I could hear Abraham behind me, cursing, and felt a hand slide across my upper arm. I didn't know if it was Derek or Abraham who reached for me, but I tugged away and kept going.

I barely reached the boy in time. My hand went out to grab him, and the whip came down over my wrist. Pain like a very hard Indian burn rose through my arm. I was pulled forward by my hand, but my shoulders were grabbed and pulled back. I couldn't help but gasp.

"How dare you — ?" the man began but stopped when a hand appeared on his shoulder.

"Pompous bastard," a deep voice said behind my right ear. "Some Gatiens jos' canna' take a joke."

I was about to turn to the boy to see if he was all right before a voice echoed around me. A voice I knew instantly. The one voice I could signal out in a crowd of people just like this and not even have to look. The voice whose owner had nearly killed me.

"Gregory, you know the penalty for assaulting a maiden?" Collin asked. He had stepped beside the Gathien, Gregory, now with his hand on the man's shoulder. Gregory was the man Cintia had spoken of. He was in charge of Weres.

"She got in my way, m'lord," the Gathien said.

"Did she now?" Collin looked at me then. His hand slid from the Gathien's shoulder, slid down his arm, and then grasped the whip. At first, I thought he was going to whip me with it, but instead, the whip went loose on my wrist and slid off. I rose my other hand and rubbed my wrist, hiding the fact that it had burned me. "Is this true?" Collin asked me. Slowly I rose my eyes to look at him. His pupils were pure black, just as they always had been. Thankfully, they didn't glow red like they usually did. But still, the hair on the back of my neck rose.

I knew I had to answer. "Yes," I replied, without removing my eyes from his.

"I do believe this maiden, as you called her, saved meh bossum from being brutally hurt, m'lord, and if I do say so myself—" the boy began.

"Shut it, mongrel. Or do you wish to join your father in the dungeons? Is he not up for a beheading sometime in the fortnight?"

The boy's voice was so familiar, yet I couldn't seem to put my finger on it. When I finally turned my head to get a look at him, my heart began to beat faster than a bee's wings. I looked back at the crowd quickly to find Abraham and Derek pushing through. Obviously, Abraham had seen the same thing because his mouth fell open into a perfect O as I turned back to the male I had saved.

"Gavin?" I asked.

CHAPTER 9

Cameron

"Have we met?" Gavin asked.

I couldn't answer him. All I could do was shake my head. There was no way this was my Gavin. How could he have come to the past too? Besides, if it was him, wouldn't he know who I was?

Abraham came to me, putting a hand out to help me up. After I took it and he pulled me up, we both turned towards Collin, who was staring at us. He didn't even blink. I didn't know what it was about the way he looked at us, but to me, it looked as if he knew exactly who we were and why we were there. That wasn't possible...I hoped. But then again, I clearly remembered him being killed. It was not exactly something I could forget.

"Go on with the party, my friends!" Collin said, and then the music and the chatter started up again. Someone touched my side, and I glanced up to see Derek standing there. He looked at Collin, unlike the way myself and Abraham were. He was actually smiling. Abraham turned from me and bent over to help up Gavin, who was sliding through the slimy food that was all over the floor.

"Collin, my good friend. I see you have spotted my guest, Anne," Derek said, putting a hand out to Collin, who took it. It was so weird hearing someone talking about me but with a different name. Anne didn't fit me at all. I was Cameron, Cameron Evans. I rubbed my arm while Derek let his hand fall from Collin's. Collin smiled then.

"I do believe she dropped in, actually. Pleasure to meet you, Anne," Collin said to me.

"Pleasure," I replied while looking at the floor. I didn't want to share a glance with Collin or even Derek. It was so uncomfortable. I'd been surrounded by dudes for a long time now, and I always seemed to get stuck in the middle every time...even when it was not about Sawyer! Boys could act more like girls than girls did. Wasn't it supposed to be the guy who was strong and the "protector"? Ugh, really.

The moment I got home, I knew exactly what was going to happen. I was going to show up at Sawyer's house, and everyone was going to surround me with questions. And then I'd have to deal with the fact that Richard wouldn't be there to welcome me home or my mom. I'd have to be told whether or not Jack was okay and if Kim and Danny were all right, wherever they were. I was not sure I'd be able to handle it. But somehow, I would have to.

"Perhaps my doctor should look at that. I believe I saw him only moments ago," Derek said, taking my hand and looking at it, and I let him. I looked down at my wrist to see a deep red line over it. I hadn't even noticed how hard the whip had struck me. I pulled my hand from him.

"Nonsense. I will have my medic look at it," Collin said before clapping his hands. In only moments a young girl no older than sixteen came to him. "Find Theodore; tell him we have an injury in the ballroom, and I, personally, request his assistance." Without even a word, the girl hurried off.

"It's not necessary. She'll be fine. A quick healer," Abraham said softly, placing a hand on my shoulder.

"You are certain? Very well," Collin said, unfazed, waving Abraham away.

"I have found her. However, she was busy and couldn't join us," Cintia said to the group when she walked up.

"Cintia Peythron, a pleasure as always," Collin said.

"How are you this evening, Sir Du Gant?" Cintia asked. It was so weird seeing her being so nice to him. I mean, sure, he didn't seem like the same guy that he was during my time, but still. She was like me, and he was a Gathien and our enemy. She was just keeping us safe.

"Very well. I was just speaking with your master and his guests. It does seem you have brought mischief into my home tonight." Collin said this to Derek, but it was Cintia who answered confidently.

"Oh, heavens no. She's just strong-willed."

Sawyer

"There's no way to bring them back?" Sawyer called. Everyone stood around the mansion as Jack slowly sat up from the couch. "They were sucked into a bright hole in the ground, and there's nothing we can do?"

"What do you expect us to do? Just make it appear? Cameron and Abraham are smart...they'll figure it out," Sander said. "Right now, we need to figure things out about Richard. We need to take his body and have it buried. Cameron would never forgive you if she knew you hadn't buried him."

An hour had passed since Cameron and Abraham disappeared into the night. Everything could have been stopped had Sawyer remembered that journal. He should have destroyed it. He should have never agreed to keep it for Jack without knowing the entire story behind it. Jack knew more than he was letting on, and this made Sawyer very angry. He charged at Jack, pulling him up from the couch. "Tell us the truth! Tell us where they went!" he growled, feeling his bones ache.

Sander took hold of Sawyer's arm and pulled it away. Shane put a hand on Jack's good shoulder to pull him back, with his other arm pulled in a sling.

"Sawyer, he's not going to be able to help you! He needs to rest! We all need to rest!" Shane said.

"Shane's right, Sawyer. We aren't going to get anywhere fighting with each other," Sander said.

Sawyer slowly put Jack back down on the couch, mortified by how he was acting. Cameron would be disappointed in him if she knew how horribly he was treating Jack. Yes, Jack knew more than he let on, but Sawyer knew deep down that no one could have known Emily's plan from the beginning. After laying Jack down, he went across the room and sat on a chair, putting his face in his hands.

"I'll call Richard's minister and make arrangements. For now, let us give him peace, and we will decide what we'll do next after that. Agreed?" Sander said behind Sawyer. Everyone nodded their agreement, and finally, Sawyer nodded too. He heard the others' feet moving until they left the room. What could he do? Where had they disappeared to? Cameron and Abraham should both be there for the burial of their stepfather.

No, their stepfather should have never been killed in the first place. Sawyer would never forgive himself if Cameron and Abraham weren't brought back. He would die for Cameron if it came down to it.

A while later, Sawyer went up to his room and lay on his bed, clothes, shoes, and all. He looked up to the ceiling, where the time clung to it reflected from the clock on the bedside. It was only ten, but it seemed much later than that. He could hear Sander's muffled voice from the room across the hall until he fell asleep.

A few days later.

"Jack isn't going to be there, is he?" Sander asked.

Sawyer leaned up against the wall in the entrance of his home. "No, he's sleeping everything off," he replied, letting out a deep sigh as he rubbed his face. It was quiet for a few minutes as the boys got themselves together. Shane was in Sawyer's room trying on a few suits to see which one fit best while Sander finished tying his shoe. It had been a week since Cameron went missing. Sawyer had been responsible for making up an explanation for Richard's death. The police were told that when the boys arrived, Richard had been on the ground with a bookshelf on top of him, thus causing his neck to be broken. It had been a horrible couple of days.

"And what do we do?" Sander asked in a whisper. Shane came down the steps messing with his tie in confusion. Sawyer looked down at his dry hands and began to rub them together. "Just go to this and act like nothing's happened? What do we say to everyone?"

"I honestly don't know, Sander. Cameron and Abraham should be here for the funeral. I don't think Danny's mom is believing us that they needed to get away for a while," Sawyer said, following Sander and Shane into the kitchen to grab a water from the refrigerator. Kingsley sat at the table, waiting patiently for them.

"They could be hurt," Sander said in a tone that reminded Sawyer of a child when they didn't get their way. "Or worse."

Sawyer growled, "Don't you think I know that? If you have a plan, let's hear it!"

The front door came open, then was slammed. Sawyer and Sander rose to their feet instantly, uncertain of who might have just entered their house. Determined footsteps came down the hall, followed by two voices. Once they came into view, both of the boys let out a breath. The familiar faces both smiled at them when they reached them, the female throwing her arms around Sawyer and Sander.

"Kim, what are you doing here?" Sander asked as he and Sawyer pulled from her grasp.

Kim let go. "You don't honestly believe that I'm going to stay away while my best friend is gone and her stepfather is dead? No, definitely not." Kimmeh was wearing tan shorts that nearly matched her dark skin, a pale pink cover shirt which made her hair look darker than normal, and Skechers... not what people would wear to a funeral. "Do you have any news?" Kim asked. Her smile faded into a flat line, waiting for someone to answer. She began to braid her hair to the side.

"Not a thing," Shane said from behind them, shaking hands with Danny, whose muscles seemed to have grown twice as large. "Sawyer hasn't even felt any emotion from her since she left."

"Yes, thank you, Shane," Sawyer said, glaring at him.

"Sorry, but it's true."

"I can't believe — well, no, I actually can believe that Emily did this. Murdering Cameron and Abraham's stepdad. They must be hurting right now, wherever they are," Kimmeh said.

"If they are," Shane said.

"Shane, shut up, please," Sawyer snapped, annoyed.

"It's nearly two...we need to start heading to the church. We can discuss things afterward," Danny said, pushing his sleeve back down to cover his watch. Everyone started towards the front of the house as Shane finished tying his tie. Kim ran up the stairs to change and quickly rejoined them out front in a long black dress.

Sawyer felt helpless. There was nothing he could do to bring Cameron back, but he still had to have hope that she would come back to him. There was no way she wouldn't come back to him. He would never give up.

The ride to the church Cameron's family grew up in was a long one. When they drove up, there were many other cars parked in the parking lot, most of which Sawyer had never seen before. The only one Sawyer was familiar with was the small car owned by Danny's mother, Helen. Once Danny parked his car and Sawyer parked the truck, they met up to enter the church together. The church was quiet other than the soft cry of a woman up front, a young brunette girl rubbing the woman's shoulders. It wasn't until Danny went ahead of them with Kimmeh that Sawyer realized it was Helen who was crying and Danny's little sister comforting her. Helen stood from where she was seated and hugged Danny, placing a hand on Kimmeh's shoulder as she cried. Sawyer joined Shane and Sander in a row towards the back. He lowered his head. The casket was closed.

CHAPTER 10

Cameron

"Pardon my asking, Anne, but do you have any relatives here?" Collin asked, handing me a drink. I took it but didn't take a drink from it. I looked over at Abraham, who was chatting silently with Cintia. So much for his help.

"I am staying with an uncle," I replied.

"Ah, which uncle would you be speaking of?"

"Desperaux Davenport," Derek replied for me. Jeez, Collin made me feel so uncomfortable. But then again, I wondered if we got rid of him now, would we have a normal life? Or would that just totally be a bad idea? Life without Gathiens. Life with Richard, Mom, and if Jack was okay...no. If Collin had never existed, then Jack and Mom might not have ever met. I wouldn't have existed. I wouldn't have met Sawyer.

Sawyer...I hoped he was all right.

"Sir Davenport? The knight? Isn't he your uncle as well, Derek?"

"Step only. Anne and I have no blood relation."

"I do believe I saw your uncle not long ago. Has he remarried? I saw a very lovely creature on his arm." Collin took a deep drink of his wine while looking about the room. I snarled my nose at him.

"Not that I am aware. Perhaps who you saw was his daughter, my cousin, Miriam," Derek said.

"Perhaps, perhaps." Collin's eyes traveled around the room still. He handed his empty glass to a passing waitress and then crossed his arms behind his back. He was so different. Maybe he wasn't a killer in the beginning...but then again, why was he that way during my time if he wasn't during this time? So many questions stormed my mind.

The music changed to a slower beat, and a couple walked onto the dance floor together. Everyone else departed it, leaving the two by themselves. I watched as the couple began to dance in a very slow but nice way. I looked behind myself to see that Cintia and Abraham had stopped whispering and had their eyes on the couple too. My eyes traveled up to look at Derek, who didn't even seem to know I was there anymore. After that, I looked, very slowly, over at Collin. I jumped when I noticed he was staring right at me. I instantly looked away.

Once the song ended, the couple left the dance floor with two of their hands tightly together risen in the air. There was a thick thud to the floor that rang three times. "Sir Gaspard Du Gant and his wife to be, Zalvana Peythron!" My stomach dropped. How could she do that? Marry a Gathien? Everyone broke into applause. I slowly clapped along, looking wild-eyed at Abraham, who wasn't clapping and wasn't looking at me either. He was glaring.

"Excuse me," I said to Collin and Derek before going over to Abraham. I placed a hand on his arm...his skin was burning to my touch. "Ab?" I asked. He didn't even blink. "Ab, what is it?"

"Emily." The name sent a sharp flow of anger down my whole body. He said it so fast I almost didn't catch it. I followed his gaze. "She has no idea we're here." The bright red hair wasn't hard to miss. Her laugh was so distinct. Her hand caressed a very bulky male's chest. Angered flared in me at the sight of her. I stepped forward, but Abraham put his arm out to block me.

Sawyer

After the funeral, everyone met out front. Danny was talking with Kimmeh and his little sister while his mom dug in her car, seeming to be searching for something. "Helen wants all of us to come to her place for dinner after the burial," Sander said, coming up to Sawyer's side.

Sawyer set his jaw. It wasn't that he didn't love Helen like his own mom, but the time wasn't right. With everything going on, Sawyer didn't even want to think about food. All he could think about was Cameron and whether she was all right. Helen pulled out a bouquet of flowers.

"You guys go ahead. I think I'll just head home," Sawyer replied, looking to Sander.

"I can go with you—" Sander started.

"No, go on. I think I've had enough of funerals for a while." Sawyer smiled softly at his brother. "It's okay. Really, go ahead." Sander hesitated before jogging over to Danny's car, where Shane had crawled into the back.

Sawyer watched them until they were out of sight. Once he got into his truck, he looked back at the church. He waited there a while as everything turned quiet, and the sun moved just over the ridge. It had been years since he had been in a church, and never had he thought it would be for another funeral. The last funeral he had attended was the funeral of his own parents, who were killed by Gathiens. The day was still fresh in his mind. He had been thirteen, Kimmeh was ten, and Sander was six. They were living in Louisiana at the time. Sawyer had been sitting with his father, aunt, and uncle on a picnic blanket as his mother swam in the river with his siblings and cousin Ashley. Until that day, they had never even heard of Gathiens…they had hardly known their fates as Weres.

His father had yelled suddenly for everyone to become quiet, and his mother quickly pulled the kids from the river, rushing them to their side on the blanket, their bodies dripping with water. Sawyer had smelt it too…the smell was so distinct to him, even now. His senses warned of an unnatural scent that flowed in the air. His nostrils lifted and fell. The smell was so familiar yet so different. His hearing listened intently. It had all happened so fast. He remembered his father looking at him and telling him to run, and he'd done just that. He took his siblings and Ashley and he had run until they reached the city, where he could get ahold of a phone to call the police. His nana was the first person he saw other than the police, and it was she who had told them his parents, as well as Ashley's, had died. The truth was that Sawyer's parents, and aunt and uncle, were killed keeping the children safe from the pair of Gathiens that crossed their lands. They were only protecting them, and they'd died for it. Had it not been for Sawyer, who had gotten the younger ones out, they probably would have been dead too.

Sawyer laid his head on the steering wheel as he started the truck.

Once he got home, he parked the truck. Kingsley arrived before him and waited for him at the door, holding it open for Sawyer to enter, and once he did, the same scent rose to his senses. He could feel his teeth quiver as his Were-form ached to take over. What was this? His heart beat fast, and his nerves were shouting at him. Something was happening that he had never experienced before. He couldn't explain it.

There was a strange scent coming from the kitchen, and

Sawyer followed it. He looked back for Kingsley, who walked behind him, looking at the door with wonder. When Sawyer pushed the door open, he nearly fell back at the sight. There were at least twenty people in his kitchen, most of whom had black gowns on.

"Who are you, and what do you want?" Sawyer asked.

"We do not speak in front of those without magic." Sawyer looked over at Kingsley, whose face was pale.

"Go on, Kingsley," Sawyer said. Kingsley looked at him before hurrying out of the kitchen.

"What is your business here?" Sawyer asked again. The men and women before him moved aside, letting a man step forward. His eyes were unlike the others and were filled with a bright green that nearly matched his own, except for the very slight color of blue on the outside of his pupil. They almost reminded him of....

"Uncle?" His father's brother, whom he hadn't heard from since he was young.

"Yes," his uncle said, almost in a whisper, before looking back at the ones behind him. "We are the Council of Were, and we are not here to harm anyone." His uncle put his arms out to his sides. Sawyer didn't believe him. Nonetheless, he stood his ground and listened. "We want the girl." Appalled, Sawyer looked at the man he had once called family. He shook his head for a moment before it finally sank in. These people were the answer to Cameron's questions...they knew what Sawyer did not.

"The girl. The girl as in Cameron."

The man nodded. "It is the girl's time to go. Her brother will stay here."

"You can't have her." Did they not know Cameron and Abraham were missing?

"It is not your choice to make, Sawyer. She belongs to the

light creatures. We have a joint code for the safety of those that are not meant to be in existence any longer. She belongs to her people. Her mother demands this, so we must not break the code."

"Her mother? But her mother is —"

"Dead? I'm sure she is very well aware of this. The girl will be safe with us. Her brother, however, has been touched by darkness. He cannot come. Where is she?"

"Gone, Uncle."

"Gone?" asked a woman standing behind his uncle.

"Where she is, you can't have her...not even I can."

"What is it you speak of, Sawyer?"

"A Gathien, Emily, has taken herself, Cameron, and Abraham to hell-knows-where."

"Making up stories will not keep her from us." A woman from the back came forward. Her hair was bright as the sun, and her eyes blue as ice. "I believe if you ask her yourself, she would want to join us. We understand her, werewolf, and we can help her. Do not keep her from us."

"Why do you feel you can refer to me as werewolf? I am Sawyer Virgo, Alpha of the Virgos."

"For your name, werewolf is unworthy of being spoken by our kind," the woman spat. Sawyer growled but was shut down by his uncle, who put his hand up to silence him and the woman. Her head went down, and she backed away from him and his uncle.

"Are you saying we are enemies?" he asked his uncle.

"What you don't know is for the better. Tell us where she is, and we will leave."

"No," Sawyer growled again. How could they come into his home, uninvited, and say he and these people were enemies? How could they say Cameron's mother was...that Cameron and Abraham were his enemies too? He looked at each of the creatures, both werewolf and light creature alike. "What are you?" he asked the woman.

"The light," she said.

There was a crash at the kitchen door, and suddenly Sander and Shane came bursting in, in their Were-forms. Kingsley peeked in behind them. Sawyer turned back to find the creatures were gone, and all he found was a name written on a floating piece of paper. D. A. R. Sawyer grabbed the paper from the air and smashed it into his pocket. Shane and Sander transformed into their human forms. "What was that?" Shane asked.

"The council. It's nothing. They just wanted to see to our pack's well-being."

"All of this just to know about our well-being?" Shane scratched the back of his ear like a dog. "I don't remember Weres bursting into bright lights."

"Wait, do you smell that?" Sander asked. "I know that smell." He raced from the room. Shane and Sawyer exchanged looks before following. The front door was wide open when Sawyer and Shane reached it, and they could hear many voices. Familiar faces surrounded the front yard. One, in particular, stood out. Gavin. He raced from the crowd to reach Sawyer, who hesitantly shook hands with him.

"This is goin' to sound rally strange. But I had a very large sense of déjà vu the other day," Gavin said. His accent was less noticeable, and his face was strained.

"What do you mean?" Sawyer asked.

"I was in me home, and suddenly I slipped on water that was splashed all over the kitchen floor. I knocked over the table and fell right on me ass. You'd be surprised how many times thawt's happened to me before. But this time, when I did, I remembered someone. It wasn't a usual memory, because before I had a fight with a man and was put into stocks because of it. It was a long time ago. But this time I remembered a woman. She helped me. It's like I completely forgot about her, and I had replaced my memory with her in it. It was Camerown. Strange, isn't it?"

"You are sure you didn't dream this?"

"Completely."

It was strange. Sawyer lifted his hand to his jaw and rubbed it in thought. Maybe Gavin was just having Cameron withdrawal? How could someone's past just change? Was he simply going mad? Too much was happening at once.

CHAPTER 11

Cameron

"We need to stop her!" I said. I could feel my body burn. Abraham didn't say anything to me but kept his eyes locked on Emily. "You—" I began, but a hand was placed on my arm. I turned to find Collin standing there. He smiled at me, but I could see the fire in the back of his eyes.

"Care to have a dance?" Collin asked me. My throat tightened as I looked at him. I nodded and took his arm that he'd held out to me like he was confident I was going to say yes to him. Obviously, he always got what he wanted when it came to girls. He led me out to the dance floor, where others joined us. Neither of us said anything for a while until Collin spoke. I tried to keep my eyes from looking at him. "You are very lovely, dear Anne. It causes me to wonder why you're not taken. Or have I misread your signs with Mr. Derek...?"

"No. There's nothing going on with me and Derek. We're cousins."

"Step only, am I correct?" he asked, lowering his hand to the bottom of my spine.

"Yeah, but—"

"Very well. I have a proposal for you."

"Excuse me?" I asked, alarmed.

"A proposal. I know you have only just arrived in town, and it's a pity you don't know many here. But I have yet to have a lady to my chambers in a few nights time. One doesn't meet a foreign lady as lovely as you often."

"How dare you!" I said, more loudly than I had anticipated.

Collin wasn't fazed at all…he just continued to lead me in the dance. I looked around for Abraham or Derek, or even Cintia, but none of them were around.

"I am never disobeyed by a woman of court, Miss Anne," Collin said, almost in a whisper.

"Well, it's a good thing I'm not a part of your court, isn't it?"

This only made Collin's smile larger. I just loved how I was amusing him. I would never be with him, let alone *do* him. He may not be evil right now, but he sure as hell was being a prick. I didn't see how he thought he could have me just like that. Apparently, any girl would give themselves over to him because he was a lord. So disgusting! Gladly, the song came to an end. I tugged from his grasp, but his hands squeezed mine.

"I will not be made a fool of."

"I don't think you have a choice. Let me go!" My heart began to race and ache. I knew Collin could feel it because his smile turned into a grin, an evil grin. *There you are*, I thought. I tugged again, looking around for anyone to help me. I even looked to where Emily was before, but she was gone.

"You are a unique woman, Anne. You are strong, and those eyes. They're so bright." He got really close to me after pulling me in. "Come now…don't struggle." I looked into his eyes and saw the pupils enlarge and then shrink. Was he really trying to put me in a trance, like he had done to Abraham and Sawyer?

"I will never give myself up to a man like you!" I said. My mouth was going dry, and my hands began to burn. I looked down at them, and all of a sudden, Collin was thrown across the room. Light exploded from my palms. I gasped at the pain. It hurt so much I fell to my knees with my hands held out in front of me. This had never happened before! I couldn't help but let out a scream. There was no way of stopping it. I had no control.

"Guards! Guards!" said a deep voice. I didn't take a chance to see who it was. Instead, I got to my feet the best I could and darted towards the door. The light exploded from my hands again, causing me to drop to the floor. I cringed into a ball with a yell. I could see guards coming my way and the ballroom doors being bolted shut. Everyone was running in different directions, screaming.

"Come." I looked up to find Derek, his hands out to me. I was afraid to grab his hands with mine, so Derek grabbed me and pulled me up into his arms and then flung me over his shoulder. My palms were bleeding and black. It was like flying for a moment until I felt a shoulder shoved into my stomach.

Derek found a far door and went out before laying me down outside of the ballroom doors. It didn't take long before I heard Abraham's voice. I could still hear the hustle and bustle in the next room behind me. "Take this." I looked up to find Abraham holding out a cloth to me. I expected it to soothe my burned hands, but all it did was hold in my light.

Derek tied the cloth around my palms before pulling me into his arms once more. "Follow me! Come!" Derek yelled to Abraham.

"What about Cintia? Or Zalvana?" Abraham called. I could tell Derek was way ahead of him.

"Cintia would have left with my horses. Zalvana isn't our

problem. Gaspard will keep her safe."

There was a loud click. My eyes flew open to see Ab and a bunch of men behind him, shooting arrows at us. My head felt light, so I closed my eyes. There was a yell from behind us, and thinking it was Abraham, I opened my eyes again. But instead, I found brown shaggy hair and arms held open wide, with a shield that he had knocked two of the guards out with. When he turned around, I couldn't help but smile. Gavin was smiling his usual triumphant smile.

"A wolf helping out a pair of O'ahee creatures? I'd say this is a first," Derek said, staring at Gavin hatefully.

"Like tha say, let bygones be bygones, aye?" Gavin replied, pushing his hair back.

"Welcome aboard." Abraham shared a glance with me and then smiled. "You know the underground passages?" Derek asked.

"Well, it all depends, rally. Where ya headin'?" Gavin asked as we entered another room. He and Abraham shut the door and locked it but also put their weight against the door to keep the guards out.

"Hawtly Dinn," Derek said.

"Then you will want to go that way." Gavin signaled to the open hall that went down into darkness.

I shut my eyes instantly. I hated the dark, even if I had a light to use. But right now, I didn't really trust my light. It was just too painful.

Derek began to move again. I could hear the boys dragging their feet behind us. We went on and on, but Derek never got out of breath from holding me for so long. While we walked, I thought about what Derek had said earlier and how he'd said it to Gavin. Why did Derek act so hateful toward Gavin? Gavin was helping us.

Once Derek came to a stop, I opened my heavy eyes to

find Gavin in his Were form. Abraham stood on the other side of him. "I need to find the right soil...ah. Here we are." Derek lifted his arm from me and grabbed me by the other arm. I could hear a slight creaking noise, and then I felt the wind. Once it came completely open, we exited quickly, shut the door, and then stepped farther into the woods before us, and finally, Derek set me down. "Let me see your hands," he said, kneeling down beside me. I held my palms out to him. He pulled the cloth from my hands and examined them without touching them. "We need to medicate them. Cintia, I believe, will have a soothing potion for them. Back off," he said quickly, his eyebrows furrowed. I looked up to find Gavin leaning back like Derek had said to. After tying the cloth back around my hands, Derek spoke again. "We are only a few miles away from Cintia's home. The sun is going down." He looked up at the sky before whispering something. I thought it was a name, but I couldn't be sure.

There was a loud whistle and a bright flash, and suddenly there was an orange figure exploding from the light. The whistle got louder until it came into view. Eden flew down, landing on Derek's outstretched arm.

"Hello, lovely," Derek said. Gavin growled. Eden looked over at him and began going crazy. Her golden feathers rose like a cat's fur would when threatened. "Calm yourself, Eden. He is no threat," Derek said soothingly, rubbing the bird's back. It helped, but she still stared at Gavin with peering owlish eyes. "Come now, Eden. Lead us to Cintia's. Go on." He raised his arm and barely pushed upward, then the bird flew. It was amazing to see. Her golden feathers glowed, and her body blazed into a bright white light. Her eyes even glowed but also twinkled in a way. She was beautiful. "Can you walk?" I looked over at Derek and then stood, nodding while I did. Each of us followed the bird, and eventually, it began to get dark.

"Why don't we have a guardian flier?" Abraham asked. I was wondering the same thing. I didn't remember ever having a bright bird thing leading me home in the dark. Like when all of this started, and I had that awful night with Adam. Why didn't I have a guardian bird then?

"All O'ahee people have them. You just have to let she or he know you want their guidance. Otherwise, they don't know you need it. They're always with you." I needed guidance right now. But technically, I didn't really exist in this time, so I doubted my bird friend was here. What was I supposed to do when I got home? If I even did? Was Jack all right? Did Sawyer and the boys destroy Shaven? Were Kimmeh and Danny okay? So many questions. No answers.

We walked until we reached Cintia's hidden home. When we reached it, things were uneasy. The horses were still connected to the carriage and were very jumpy. While Derek fed and watered them, Abraham went ahead to the boulder door, and I followed. The door was partially open when we reached it. Abraham reached his good hand back and held me behind him. With his shoulder that was wrapped, he pushed the door open, and it creaked. I looked around Abraham to look inside. Everything was knocked over and trashed. Gavin climbed in, pushing Abraham and I aside, and began sniffing the ground. Derek came up behind us, holding a piece of cloth. "Cintia dropped this. She's left us a trail of scent. She must have seen the mutt coming to our aid." Derek followed Gavin and looked around before searching the back rooms. He came back with a letter. "'I was followed. Zalvana will protect me. Go into hiding. All of you. Cintia.'"

"All of us? Does sha mean me as well?" I turned to look at Gavin. His body was completely bare. I couldn't believe my eyes, and yet I couldn't help but totally let my eyes travel him up and down.

"Oh my god!" I yelled and looked away, putting my hands over my eyes. I hid my smile.

"Dude!" I heard Ab say.

"Have none of ya eva seen a naked man before? Wouldn't ye happen to have a pair of pants to spare, would ya? Mine ripped." I expected he asked Derek, even though this was Cintia's house. That reminded me...why had Cintia had men's clothing for Ab in the first place? There was a rustle of feet leaving the room, and then a few minutes later, they returned. I peeked through my fingers to find Gavin tying his pants and sighed with relief. As always, I was stuck with a bunch of men.

Derek came out of the back room with a handful of things. He handed a few of them to Abraham, then Gavin, and then began to dress himself too. I looked at them with slit eyes. "Excuse me. Where's my armor?" I asked. All of them looked at me.

"This is no place for a womun, love. Besides, isn't it yew they har after?" Gavin said.

I stood, and my arms fell to my sides.

Once Derek was fully dressed, he handed me a bottle of blue liquid. "Rub this on your hands."

I opened the bottle. A fume of blue foam floated out of it. At least I didn't have to drink it. I poured it into my hands and yelled at the pain. I dropped the bottle, and it scattered into pieces across the floor. I looked down at my hands as they bubbled and fizzed...literally! But then it smoothed out, and my skin turned back into its natural state. I moved my fingers around.

"Thanks," I said in a gasp. I hadn't even noticed I was holding my breath.

"Don't thank me. Cintia had it laid out for you."

CHAPTER 12

Cintia

Her eyes cracked open as her body was dragged. The only thing she could move was her smallest fingers. The guard's shoes echoed as they stomped down the hallway. Her blurry vision stung when they entered a bright room. There were many voices around her, but the only voice she listened for was her sister's.

Then she heard a laugh…a very feminine, soft laugh that was cut off by the clap of a hand as if someone had clasped a hand over the person's mouth. The laughing all around stopped in an instant and was replaced by gasps. There was a clatter of feet, and then small hands were placed on Cintia's cheeks. Her face was lifted, and her cheek was rubbed.

"What is this?" Zalvana called. Her voice was strong. "I say! Why is my sister hurt?" She was asking the guards. "Cintia, darling, can you hear me?"

Through a bruised and swollen mouth, Cintia replied, "Yes."

A door opened and closed, and then there was a loud clash of men's voices yelling at each other, two of whom Cintia knew…Collin and his father, Gaspard. "I saw the girl with my own eyes, Collin! Cintia Peythron was nowhere near them! Many were afraid and left in a rush. The girl simply was one of *them*. Even some of our friends fled during the scene. Will you have their heads put upon spikes as well?"

"My sister, look at her! Who did this?" Zalvana called again. There was silence. Cintia barely opened her eyes to see Gaspard glaring at Collin, with his arm around Zalvana's shoulders.

"My prat of a son had his guards bring her to the dungeons for associating with an O'ahee woman. I had her brought from the dungeons the moment I heard of it," Gaspard said calmly.

"The dungeons?" Zalvana asked, appalled, as she reached for Cintia. "Let me have her." The guards stood their ground. "Gaspard, let me heal her," Zalvana pleaded, looking back at Gaspard with sadness. "She needs to be healed."

"Of course. You may take her to our chambers while I speak with the court."

"Thank you."

Zalvana kissed her fiancé before taking Cintia and helping her walk through the Du Gant home until they reached a very large bedroom, one so big it made Cintia's home look like a pebble in the middle of a pile of boulders. Cintia was sat on a deep velvet bed while Zalvana hurried over to fill a pot with water and placed it halfway over a nearby fire that blazed in the fireplace. The guards left the room, shutting the door behind them.

"Oh, my dear sister," Zalvana said while she placed a cloth in the pot when it began to boil. Once she pulled the cloth out of the water, she pulled the pot off the fire with a glove and then waited until the cloth was cool to give it to Cintia. "Clean yourself," Zalvana said, handing it to her. Cintia did the best she could. Feeling came back to her hands. "I never thought you would run from your people, C." Zalvana went over to a small table that she lifted to pull out a box tied underneath it. She placed the box on the table and pulled out a yellow leaf, crushed it, and then poured it into the same pot she had used for Cintia's cloth. "It's not like you."

"I had no choice," Cintia mumbled.

"Everyone has a choice. Something is up with you. Dear sister, tell me, who was that girl? She looked strangely familiar when I saw her running from the hall."

"She looks like you and me. A sister of our kind. She is not used to Collin's ways. I believe Collin wanted her to accompany him to his room. She was frightened, is all."

"And now he will want her because she refused. That is how he is." *Or perhaps because she looked just like you*, Cintia thought. "I fear she will be executed, that girl."

"They will have to find her first," Cintia said. Zalvana whistled. A moment later, a bird much smaller than her own, Edenaun, yet just as beautiful, flew into the open window. The bird landed on the table next to Zalvana, its bright eyes looking at Zalvana with respect and protection.

"I need your tears, Meson," Zalvana said, holding out a small cup. Meson leaned her very small face over the cup and squinted her eyes. A few drops of gold fell from her eyes and into the cup. "Thank you, my girl." After petting her, Zalvana stirred the liquid, dipped the cup into the water with the leaf, and then brought it over to Cintia. "Drink this. You will heal much quicker."

"Thank you." She drank the potion in one gulp, and her body instantly felt fresh and renewed. "You will not tell, will you?"

"Of course not!" Zalvana replied. "But I do suggest you stay out of the Du Gant's eyes till all of this passes. I cannot help you again. I need to keep myself on a straight line with Gaspard, you hear? So that I may become pregnant soon."

"Are you sure you wish to do this, Z?" Cintia asked, handing her the empty cup. Zalvana was silent while she took the cup and laid it on the table. She then returned to Cintia's side and took the cloth from her, and began to rub Cintia's swollen face.

"I am," Zalvana said finally. "Someone needs to make things better. And if I am capable of doing so, then I will. Think of how powerful my child would be, C! Part Gathien and part O'ahee. She would be so strong. The powers of a Gathien and the light gift of an O'ahee! Can you imagine?"

"He will kill you. The moment that child is born and glows for the first time, he will have you beheaded. And then what? He will kill your child with you. I could not bear it."

"I have a plan for that." Zalvana looked at her sister then. "The moment that day comes, everything that was once mine will be yours, including my child. You hear! You will raise my child as your own. It is your burden to not be able to have children. I trust you."

Sawyer

Everyone sat silently in the living room, thinking over everything that had happened, trying to put the pieces together. There had to be an answer...an answer that did not want to be found. Sander sat with Rebecca, Gavin's younger sister, Danny and Kim sat together, and everyone else sat with at least one partner. Except Sawyer, who sat in his chair in front of the fireplace.

"Maybe they are in a different country," said Kyle. His hair was now shaved off on the opposite side of his head, and a streak of green ran through the braided hair on the other side.

"She would have called then, wouldn't she? That can't possibly be it," his mate, Abigail, replied.

"You say you believe this Emily wishes to kill Cameron's ancestry? What if they went to when their family was alive? What about that Zalvana woman?" Rebecca asked.

"Yes, that makes a lot of sense, Becca. But how did they accomplish that?" Abigail said. Sawyer looked over at Rebecca. Sander's arm was over her shoulders, patting her arm softly. The two youngest wolves in the packs.

"The journal," Gavin said, looking at the floor. "Jack had you hide this journal from her. Did he ever say why?"

Sawyer looked to him and replied. "He only told me it was important. Is he up, Kingsley? He needs to explain himself." Kingsley said nothing but left the room. Jack had been staying in their guest room since the night Cameron and Abraham had disappeared, and he was slowly getting better.

"And you have no feeling of her?" Gavin asked.

"We wouldn't be sitting here if I did," Sawyer replied, a bit annoyed at his question.

The double doors came open, and Kingsley walked in with Jack right behind him. He was very pale, and his eyes changed from brown to black.

"What do you need?" Jack asked huskily.

"We would like to know as much as possible about this journal," Gavin said.

Sawyer looked at Gavin with a snarl. Jack rubbed his face as Sander and Rebecca slid down the couch so Jack could sit down. He thanked them before he began.

"The journal didn't belong to me. The journal had been passed down for generations through the Peythron line. The original owner of the journal was, as you know, Zalvana Peythron. Thank you." Kingsley handed him a water, which he took a sip from before continuing. Sawyer shook his head at Jack as he told them the information that would have helped them from the beginning. "Zalvana was the second to the youngest of six. There was Katherine, I believe it was her name, Fiona, Jamie, Harren, Zalvana, and then Cintia, all of which were of pure blood. I never knew what it was exactly. But I did know it had something to do with light. Jules was able to do the same things Cameron and Abraham can, but she didn't want to use her abilities. She put them aside to make sure Cameron and Abraham had a normal life. That is when we decided it wasn't safe for me to be around them because of my Gathien part. Because I was only of half Gathien blood, I was able to stop the change, but we didn't know how it would affect them because they were of light and of Gathien already. We feared it would harm them. But when Jules passed away, the journal disappeared but reappeared when I found out about Abraham being changed. I met your father, the three of you before Cameron was two, and he insisted we make an alliance. He promised me his help. But he...." He looked over at Sander, then to Kim, and finally to Sawyer. "He and your mother passed away. A very tragic accident. He left me the information about his children. All of you were so young then, and I found you all still lived in the Virgo mansion. I finally decided to come to find you, Sawyer, and have you watch over Cameron for me, seeing that you both were nearly the same age and all. This was many years later. I gave you the journal to hide. I pleaded with you to protect her." He glanced around at everyone as they watched him. "I tried to keep myself from Cameron because I feared I would cause her harm. I had letters, though, that Jules had stashed away at our Virginia estate. I've thought about it—" He coughed and took another sip of water. "Gathiens of pure blood can live very long lives. As long as your parents are of Gathien blood, you become a Gathien at puberty no matter what. This was only a myth since, as you see, I'm not a Gathien. I was not pure. The bloodline of Jules was much stronger for Cameron and Abraham, but the Gathien gene took Abraham because he was surrounded by Gathiens. And thus Cameron's change after that. Anyways, the journal. I remember when Jules was alive how she would talk about her past. The journal was important to her. It belonged to Zalvana Peythron. So if we're right about Zalvana, then she had a child with a pure Gathien, hence starting the Peythron line. In the journal, Jules told me a lady in waiting took the child to its room when it was born, and the servant and the child were never seen again. That's all I know."

"They don't know who she was?" Rebecca asked.

"Jules would never tell me. But the child lived, or else Jules, Cameron, and Abraham wouldn't be here. The lady in waiting had to have known Zalvana. Possibly even planned this with her before the birth. The one person she trusted more than anyone. The last family member alive at that time. There's only one best guess…Cintia Peythron, Cameron and Abraham's great aunt. If Emily wished to kill Zalvana and they reached the past in some way, then I fear if she succeeds in killing Zalvana before the child is born, then Cameron and Abraham will have never existed. Everyone would be under the control of Gathiens just as they planned. Or what Collin planned, at least."

"It all connects! No wonder Collin wanted to get with Cameron so badly," Kim said. Everyone looked at her. "Honestly, don't you see? Collin knew Zalvana. Maybe even loved her! Maybe Cam looks just like Zalvana. Drove him mad."

"That would be so romantic if it wasn't so messed up," Rebecca said. Sander looked over at her, shaking his head.

"Abraham said Collin and Emily were related to them because Collin's father 'bedded their grandmother.' Collin's father was the Gathien," Sander said.

"Jack, I have brought me pack here because I was conflicted," Gavin began. Jack looked over at him while he drank his water. "I already told Sawyer this, but I believe it will make more sense te ye. I was at me home, and suddenly I slipped on water that was flooded all over tha kitchen floor. I knocked over the kitchen table and fell right on my ass. It's happened before. But this time when I did I remembered someone. It wasn't a usual memory, because before in this memory I had a fight with a man and was put into stocks because of it. It was a long time ago, but I remember that day perfectly. This time I remembered a woman. She helped me instead. It's like I completely forgot about her, and I had replaced my memory without her in it. It was Cameron. What do you think?"

"If they are in the past, then they have messed with something that involves your past. But if they are in Zalvana's time, I don't see how it would affect you—"

"If they are in the past, then how are we supposed to save them?" Rebecca interrupted, looking over at Gavin before flashing her eyes back over to Jack, grabbing his attention. Everyone was silent.

"Could vone of us beh sent back too?" Sam, a member of Gavin's pack, asked.

"How are we supposed to do that if we don't know how?" Sawyer asked.

"Oh...true," Sam replied.

"We will somehow need to contact a warlock. That's the only thing I can think of. But we are limited these days on warlocks," Jack said.

"I thought they were extinct," Abigail said.

"Wait, I thought witches didn't exist," Sander stated.

"No, no. Witches are not real, but warlocks are. There are still some lurking around. They live a long time. They don't do potions, brew in a cauldron and spells like witches are supposed to do," Jack said.

"I know one," Gavin said.

"You do? Well then, why didn't you bring up this warlock before?" Sawyer asked sarcastically.

"Because I didn't know Cameron and Abraham were in the past. Jack, you wouldn't happen to have a phiodinal, would you?" Gavin asked.

"I do. Why?" Jack replied, handing his empty cup to Kingsley.

"I'll need to borrow it if ye don't mind."

Jack stood and left the room. Sawyer sat and watched as everyone chatted. He should be thinking of Cameron and how she was doing, but instead, all he could think about was the strange creatures who had come to him. Their pitch white eyes had sent shivers down his spine. But why did only that one guy not have yellow eyes? Why did his uncle come, of all people? His uncle was estranged from the family long ago. How did they know Cameron's mother if she was dead? Why did they want Cameron and not Abraham? It wasn't her time to go. Nor were they going to take her from him. Never. And if anyone went back to the past to get Cameron, it would be him.

"Here." Jack came back into the room and handed Gavin a very small, deep purple whistle. Sawyer leaned in like everyone else to get a look at it.

"I'll need all of you to move to the other side of the room. I don't know where he'll end up," Gavin said. Everyone moved except Shane, whose head was tilted to the side.

"Where he'll end up?" Shane asked, but before he got an answer, Gavin blew into the whistle. A high-pitched screech exploded into Sawyer's ears. There were shrieks, and Sam dropped to his knees and possibly even fainted. A pitch-black square filled in the space between the double doors. Sawyer kept his eyes on it.

"'What is your problem? Why am I being called here?" A man stepped out of the portal. He wore old-fashioned clothes, and his shoulder pads were twice the size of his shoulders. His hair was white and went past his waist, and his eyes were gray. Sawyer couldn't help but smirk. "Don't you smirk at me, boy. I'll turn you into a toad!" he said to Shane, who must have been thinking the exact same thing Sawyer was…except Shane's smirk instantly fell when the man yelled at him. This made Sawyer chuckle.

"Phillius! You haven't aged a bit!" Gavin said, going over to the man with a hand held out. But Rebecca beat him to it. She threw herself at the old man, who returned the embrace with a laugh. His old and saggy hand patted Rebecca's head before shaking Gavin's hand.

"It has been what? Two hundred years? Maybe longer, maybe less? My old tired body can't remember. Dear Rebecca, you have grown! Heh. Look at you."

"I think your years are off. Rebecca is only sixteen," Sander said.

Phillius looked over at him, clapping his hands together. "Preferably speakin' to Gavin. But good insight, pooch. What have you called me here for, Gavin?" Phillius placed an arm over Rebecca's shoulders. Gavin didn't seem fazed a bit by the inappropriate gesture.

"We have a Gathien problem, and possibly a light people problem as well. Have any warlocks been speakin'?" Gavin asked.

"There have been rumors that the eldest Gathien to this day was killed. Though we all have participated in that. What other Gathien do you speak of?"

"Collin's sister, Emily. There had been some killings, all

meant to lead us in a different direction. However, Emily was determined to get ahold of a journal."

"Zalvana's journal."

"You know if it?"

"Well, yes, of course. Zalvana an' I go way back. She had me place a charm on the journal."

"You? What kind of charm?"

"Attachment. Bound by blood, Zalvana's journal was passed down to her sister."

"Can you be a little more specific?" Kim asked.

"The charm, young poochy, was to keep the journal hidden. Whenever it is lost, when someone says the name of Zalvana Peythron, it will return to her. Make more sense?"

"So Cameron and Abraham were taken back to Zalvana? But how was me memory changed if it was taken back to Zalvana? I was never associated with 'er during my time," Gavin said.

"At the time, charms were less achievin' than nowadays. Even I can't be perfect. It is possible the journal took the young light creatures to the year I placed the charm on the journal. Zalvana was the only Peythron I blood attached the journal to."

"How did you know about Cameron's light?" Sawyer asked.

Phillius looked at him then. His eyes were calm and understanding in a way that made Sawyer wonder. Had this man gone through so much that he was wiser than most men that lived now?

"You are pack leader, yes?"

"Yeah, so I'd advise you to answer my question."

Phillius smiled. "Of course. You are unaware of the old creatures? Gavin, I am surprised you have never told them this yourself. Ah, no, you cannot, can you?"

"I never put two and two together. I believed she and her brother were simply very powerful Gathiens. I was never close to the Peythron's. Cameron is an Evans," Gavin said.

"Indeed. Well, I knew Zalvana. To answer your question, doggy leader, Zalvana and Cintia were of O'ahee blood. The light creatures. O'ahee means light. Light means power. Power means to succeed. To succeed means to create somethin' more powerful than anything ever created."

"You're telling me the stories my wife told me were true?" Jack asked.

"Who is the wife you speak?"

"Jules Peythron, naturally."

"The Peythrons have always been women." Phillius nodded his head at his own comment.

"But I did not only have a daughter. I had a son too."

"A son? That is very odd indeed. You are of Gathien blood."

"Yep. All boys."

"Interesting. Well, you lot, how may I be of service? You have me very intrigued."

"Is there any way to send someone to the past?" Danny asked.

"No," Phillius replied instantly.

"No?"

"I cannot send one to the past without an object of someone from the past. Now, unless you happen to have a piece of Zalvana's journal...."

"Would anything from Zalvana's journal have disappeared too if the journal did?" Kim asked then.

"Not entirely...." Phillius looked over at Jack, who looked very uneasy, leaning far down into the couch.

"Excuse me," Jack said, almost in a whisper as he stood from the couch and headed for the door. The doors slammed shut, blocking him from exiting. Everyone looked at Phillius in a slight panic but quickly eased as they looked at Jack's back. Phillius let go of Rebecca's shoulder and took a few steps forward towards Jack.

"In your wallet lays a piece of parchment. Give it to me," Phillius said, holding his hand out. "Or are your children not important to you?"

Jack turned to him, placing his hand into his back pocket, and pulled out his wallet.

"Give it to him, Jack," Danny said, looking at Jack with furrowed eyebrows. "Give it to him."

After opening the wallet, Jack slowly pulled out a piece of brown-looking paper and handed it to Phillius reluctantly. Phillius yanked it back and unfolded it with an eyebrow raised.

"You have many secrets, Jack. This is merely one of them." Sawyer couldn't see what was on the paper since Phillius quickly folded it back. "Who will be sent back?"

"I will," Sawyer said.

"No, Sawyer, you can't. The pack needs you," Kim said, pushing forward from Danny's grasp.

"Cameron needs me."

"Let me go," Kim pleaded.

"No, Kim," Sawyer growled. Kim placed herself back in the seat. Another growl was made, and it took Sawyer by surprise to find it was Danny who growled at him, protecting that which was his.

"Why don' I go?" Gavin asked.

"That would be a sight!" Phillius laughed. "Two Gavins running around!"

"Two Gavins?" Sawyer asked.

"You really haven't filled them in, have ya, Gavin?" Phillius asked.

"A protector cannot speak of his past; you know this, Phillius."

"But you told me your past changed," Sawyer said.

"I told you something that happened often. Cameron has messed with me. Every other moment I get a sense of déjà vu. I can' believe I never put two an' two together," Gavin replied.

"You were too busy breaking your bond with Cameron. Why were you so intent on cutting your bond with her?" Sander asked, staring at Gavin. Then everyone followed. Gavin stared back, unfazed.

"I know what you all hare thinkin', but I am not tha bad guy here. Being a protector, I am limited on what I can tell you. If anything, maybe we should worry about ye, young one. Ye awfully quick at blaming me!"

"Be quiet!" Phillius yelled. His hair turned a bright red. Everyone went quiet just as he'd said. "It's no wonder I keep my fat old ass out of Were's business. Who here has a very close relationship with the girl? Whose known her longest?"

"Danny," Kim said quickly.

"I grew up with Cameron," Danny said. "She's my best friend."

"Good, good, you come here." Danny stood from the couch, letting Kim's hand fall from his own. Once he got to Phillius's side, Phillius placed a hand on his shoulder.

"I will go after my Cameron!" Sawyer stood.

"Think of her," Phillius said, ignoring Sawyer's outburst. Danny's eyes closed as if in a trance.

"Stop!" Sawyer roared. There was a loud crash and then a bright flash of light. Danny was thrown, and everyone moved back. Sawyer ran to the window. The edges were melting. Sawyer smelled the air.

Sawyer turned to find a bright ball of light. Everyone

stared at it except Sander, who was looking at Sawyer. Phillius fell to his knees with his hands held out in front of him. It took a moment for Sawyer to notice the fire in his fireplace was fuming.

"What the hell?" Shane said, standing from the couch. His hand was held out to the light to touch it, but the moment he touched it, he yelled in surprise. "It bit me! The light thing actually bit me!"

"It burnt you, idiot," Danny said, standing from the ground. Kim was at his side.

"What is it?" Rebecca asked. "Phillius?"

"Very powerful light," Phillius muttered.

"Powerful light?" Shane asked, wide-eyed. He gulped, taking a step back from the light.

"We've come for the girl," the ball echoed.

Sawyer was the first to speak. "I told you that you can't have her!"

"You have no choice. It is her time."

"Time for what?" Sander asked. Sawyer lifted a hand to silence him.

"To join her people," the bright light ball said. Sawyer took a few steps forward. The voice was not a male's voice anymore, but a woman's.

"Jules?" Jack asked, taking a few steps forward.

CHAPTER 13

Sawyer

No one moved. The ball of light flashed again but brighter this time. It was so bright it blinded Sawyer for a second. When his eyes cleared, what he saw shocked him more than anything. A woman stood in front of him. Her hair hung past her waist in thick waves. Her eyes glowed a bright green, and her face was pure and glowed just like the rest of her body. Sawyer then noticed her hands were cupped together, and she was smiling…a very faint smile, but it was there. Jack had stood and moved in front of Sawyer to face the woman.

"You must let her go, Jack," she said.

"How many times do I have to say it? You can't have her, so get back into that little light bubble of yours and get out of my house!" Sawyer yelled. Jules didn't make any gesture of hearing him at all. When she turned her face towards Sawyer, her eyes brightened almost enough that the green was not visible anymore.

"I have tolerated your people long enough. I am surprised Jack let it stand for so long."

"They aren't our enemies, Jules…they are the children of Reginald and Mary. You remember them, don't you?" Jack asked, almost pleading.

"Friends of yours, not mine. And I will not let my baby girl be hurt by one."

"If anything, I think it's Cameron who can hurt Sawyer," Shane said with a grin. Everyone glared at him except Jules, who continued to look at Sawyer as if he were an insect.

"My people were powerful once, and I put my powers aside so Cameron and Abraham could live normal lives. But you came and ruined it all," she said to Sawyer, whose nostrils flared.

"We protected her from Collin! He would have taken her to the dark side—" Sawyer began.

"Silence!" Jules yelled, pointing a finger at Sawyer, whose throat tightened. He was unable to speak. Jules then placed her fingertips on her temples as if she had a headache. "Where are they? Where is Cameron? My guardians tell me she will not come to me."

"Your grandmother's journal—" Jack said but was interrupted by Jules's outburst.

"What have you done?"

Cameron

When we arrived at Derek's home, we were shocked to find several guards standing around it. Derek hid me, Abraham, and Gavin in a nearby underground shelter outside his garden. I peeked through the door with Abraham and Gavin behind me, chatting about their plans to get Cintia back. Derek entered the house with a few guards following. "Would you guys shut up? I'm trying to listen for Derek," I said, throwing them a glare.

"What do you expect him to do? Yell 'come help me, my dear Anne!'? We need to stay here," Abraham said.

"What is your deal?" I replied, slowly letting the door

come down and latch on the hooks. "We have to help him and Cintia."

"Gavin here, and I have a plan already."

"If it has to do with something about leaving me behind, you'd better rethink your plan," I snapped. There was a grumble and then silence. We waited, and then finally we heard a rumble of voices. I went over to the trap door and pushed it open to take a look. Derek was being pulled out of his house in chains. All because of me. Always because of me. I began to climb out until my dress was pulled, and I fell back into the shelter. Gavin placed a hand over my mouth as Abraham peeked out. When he lowered the door, he crawled down to us. I pushed Gavin away from me.

"We need to talk to Zalvana," Abraham said.

"I thought it was too dangerous," I hissed.

"No. I think she's exactly who we need to talk to right now. Somehow when Emily called out Zalvana's name, it brought us back to when she lived, right? Well, what if Zalvana gave the journal to one of us? Or even both of us? Wouldn't it send us back home?"

"I never thought of it that way!" I said, a little disappointed in myself. But then I thought about it. "Well, wait. If we owned it, and every time we say our names, it brings itself back to us, it would be pointless, wouldn't it? Since where we are right now isn't *home*."

"We'll never know till we try."

"What about a warlock?" Gavin asked. Abraham and I looked over at him.

"A warlock?" Abraham asked.

"My friend Phillius is a warlock. Maybay he could send ye back to where ye came from?"

"I never thought of that. They don't exist in our time, do they C...Anne?"

"Not that I know of. We can't leave yet, though. We have to make sure Emily doesn't get to Zalvana," I said.

"We'll have to destroy her." The tone in Abraham's voice when he said that made me go quiet. I hadn't really thought about it, but Abraham must have a lot going on in his head. Not only did he "date" Emily and "love her," but he was tricked by her in the very beginning to switch onto Collin's bad side. His anger was being held in, but I knew it would explode from him some time. Sometime soon. It was weird to think that we were going to kill our great, great aunt. What a loving family we were. Loving, and so messed up. "When can you call this warlock?"

"As quick as a whistle."

When the warlock appeared, he was pissed. His hair fell down his back in blond waves, and he was dressed in a golden suit. "I am not in this war, Gavin!" he yelled while he plucked things from inside his clothes. I bent my head to the side to see where all of those things were coming from, but there was nothing but a little pocket. He wasn't a warlock... he was insane. He threw a vial at me, and I dropped to my knees, hearing it crash against the wall behind me. "So sorry, miss," I heard him say before I glared up at him.

"This isn't part of a war! Techniclay, they aren' even from this time."

After explaining everything that had happened, the warlock sat in thought.

"Everything is indescribable! I don't know you well, Gavin, but I can see where you're fightin' at. We save two people from bein' killed, kill a Gathien from the future, and then send these two back to where they came from. Am I correct?"

"Right, Phillius," Gavin replied.

"Are you mad?!" the warlock yelled.

"Just a little," Gavin grinned. I couldn't help but smile too.

"Right now, all we need is to know you're in," Abraham added, moving to Gavin's side.

There was a long silence. I pushed myself from the ground and brushed off my gown. There were already bunches of rips and stuff in it, and I felt bad. It was given to me by Derek, and now look where he was. I looked over at the warlock as he rubbed his beard.

"Well, of course, I'm in! Gaspard has been a thorn in my side for ages. Believe me...ages."

"Have you been to Gaspard's house lately?" I asked. The warlock looked over at me.

"I have. An' by the looks of it, you are the O'ahee girl that Gaspard's son Collin is looking for."

"Looking for?" Abraham asked.

"Oh yes. He has every guard out lookin' for her. While I was there, today actually, I saw them guards dragging in Cintia Peythron, I do believe. I think they took her to the courts. Zalvana will be there."

"You know Zalvana?" I asked.

"Of course I know Zalvana! Who doesn't know the girl is trying to trick the Gathien king Gaspard other than him? Anyway. This Derek you speak of, I am uncertain. The only help I would be to him would be if I brought you to court. Tomas, the court jester, would be no help to us there. He's terrified of Gaspard," he said to me.

"Me? But he wants me...."

"Exactly."

"I won't let him have my sister," Abraham said, taking a step towards me. He placed both of his hands on my shoulders and pulled me back a step. I looked up at the warlock, shaking my head.

"Then I guess your friend will lose his head," Phillius said.

"They can't do that!" I blurted before slamming my hands against my mouth.

"They will, I assure you. I wouldn't be surprised if they are setting up the stage right now. He's considered a traitor now."

"If he dies…." I said, still shaking my head. "If she dies…."

Abraham looked at me. "They won't. It'll mess up our whole future if Cintia dies. We'll have to free Derek and her. You'll have to do this. Let's get some rest. We have a long day ahead of us."

CHAPTER 14

The next day.

Cameron

Just before the day was to transfer to the evening, Phillius had me put on tight men's clothing and flat *Three Musketeer*-style boots. His house was very big, and most of his furniture was woven in purple and gold. We had come to his house early this morning, and with everything that had happened that day, all I wanted to do was sleep. It was an ugly awakening when Abraham woke me up before dawn that morning. Not to mention that now I almost looked like a female pirate.

After we had all of our plans set, Phillius brought us to the Du Gant's residence in his carriage. We all peeked through the woods. My heart was beating fast. I thought that by now, I wouldn't be scared over these things anymore, but I was. It never seemed to end.

"Come," Phillius said, looking back at me after pulling the carriage to a stop. I rubbed my hands on my pants, climbed out of the wagon, and walked with him out of the woods. We walked straight up to the front door.

Before Phillius knocked on the door, he turned to look at me, and with a flick of the finger, shackles flew from a bucket next to the door and bound my wrists. I couldn't believe my eyes. I felt like a prisoner. Then something else appeared...black gloves that showed the tops of my fingers. "You, m'dear, are like an untrained dragon. Those gloves will keep you from spouting fire." I didn't even want to ask. After a hard knock, we waited. Everything was so quiet. I looked back at the woods to see if I could find Abraham or Gavin, but neither were there. "I put a charm on you, so do not fear," he said quickly.

The door came open, and I turned back to it. It was the same man from yesterday. "Yes?"

"I have captured the girl. A rather fancy one, if I might add." Phillius pulled me forward by my chains to show me off. I looked at the ground, and then I was pulled forward into the house. The last time we had entered the house from the back, which had led right into the ballroom. This time we came in from the front. The whole place was dark; it almost reminded me of the inside of Hogwarts from the *Harry Potter* series. I was a big *Harry Potter* fan.

A lot of chatter echoed down the hallway. I looked around Phillius to find a group of women coming our way. Phillius didn't give them a glance as we passed them, but they were really interested in him. I tried not to look at them either.

"Who is she?" one of them asked. "She's nothing, a prisoner; come sissy." I wanted to turn around and give them a piece of my mind, but I was caught off guard when Phillius stopped, and I walked right into him. He grunted and looked down at me. I tried to smile, but he shook his head, and my smile faded.

"Don't say a word," he said before turning from me and continuing to walk behind the man. My lips clamped together like a zipper.

We entered a large room. "Phillius, m'boy! I hear you

have brought us a girl." I glanced around Phillius to an older man with a beard that was covered in grey and traveled down his chest. His hair went just below his ear lobes, and his eyes were dark. He looked like Collin. This had to be Gaspard.

"I found this one hidin' in my pumpkin patch. A pumpkin couldn't be this pretty."

"Indeed. Fetch Collin," Gaspard said to the man who had led us here, and he hurried from the room. Everyone kept talking and laughing, but Gaspard didn't join them. Neither did he give me a look. There was a loud bang that sounded like pots being thrown, and then a voice.

"I told you I didn't want to be disturbed! Now, look what you've done! I've completely lost it! My whore will not be pleased!" I looked over at Collin when he entered. His hair was messy, and his clothes were lazily thrown on. The moment he entered, his eyes set on me. "You found her!" he yelled.

"This is her then? The light child," Gaspard asked.

"Yes. I could never forget such a face. She is nothing like the women around here. Her attitude sets her apart from all others."

I clenched my teeth. Phillius shared a glance with me before looking at the crowd.

"I do believe my business is done here, m'lord," Phillius said.

"Yes, yes. Go on." Gaspard waved him away.

Phillius bowed to him and then turned to me and took the shackles off me. I looked up at him just as he looked down at me. Once the shackles clicked and he pulled them from me, he walked out of the room.

"She is something, Collin. Her looks are very peculiar," Gaspard continued. There was a click of a door behind me, and then my jaw unlocked. I licked my dry lips. "You have what you want, son. You may take her now. But I suggest a guard or two waiting outside your door. You never know what an O'ahee girl will do. Do not speak of this to Zalvana, you hear?"

A hand took hold of my shoulder, and I was pulled back. Collin had a hold of me and pulled me with him out of the room. Guards walked behind me as Collin walked ahead. The sound of footsteps echoed against the wall. I glanced into a room, and my eyes widened. Cintia sat on a bed talking to someone whose back was facing me.

"Come on!" Collin yelled, and a guard pushed me. I gave him a sharp glare and moved my feet again. At least I knew Cintia was fine and clearly not dead. But who was she talking to? Could that have been Zalvana?

Finally, we reached a two-door frame that was pushed open by Collin. He moved aside, and I couldn't look at him as I passed. He whispered something to the guards, and then the doors were shut. I stood near a small table at the end of his bed, my hands stuck together. I could hear Collin moving around behind me. I would rather die than be violated by my own blood. My breathing began to get heavy, and my hands became numb.

Abraham

"Could you be any more of a cat?" Abraham asked, looking over at Gavin, who was licking his paws while in Were form. Gavin let out a puff and let his paw fall to the ground. When Phillius came out of the building, he instantly went to them. He looked uneasy.

"Collin took her to his chambers. Even with the charm, I can't hear them," Phillius said. Abraham looked back at Gavin once again, who got to his feet.

"She's a very stubborn girl, so I know she won't let Collin

do anything to her. We need to get Derek, and quickly. We heard some guards talking while they…well, took a whiz over there, and we got some clothes." Abraham then looked over at Gavin as he pounced over with clothes in his mouth.

"Brilliant," Phillius said, pulling the clothes from Gavin's mouth, and suddenly Gavin was human again.

After they changed, they dragged the nude men deep into the woods by their feet. "You sure no one will notice you?" Abraham asked while Phillius threw leaves and branches all over the men's bodies. Gavin sat down.

"I'm a warlock. I make things happen."

Once they had everything situated and no guards in sight, they all entered the courtyard on the opposite side of the home, where they found a few women sitting on a bench. Gavin looked at them with a grin before hurrying ahead… towards the women. *Why couldn't Gavin back at home be like this one*? Abraham asked himself. By the time Abraham and Phillius reached him, he was sitting on the girls' laps, having his hair played with.

"Are these your friends?" the blonde asked.

"They are rather cute, aren't they? Which one do you want, sissy?" asked the brunette.

"Hmm." The redhead tilted her head. "I prefer the blonde." Abraham looked over at Phillius, whose whole appearance had changed. He had changed his hair into a very dull blonde, and his face was a little dirty.

"Who did you say you were looking for, love?" asked the blonde who was playing with Gavin's hair.

"My sister. She's a short little girl with long brown hair, or perhaps you could lead me to the dungeons?" Gavin asked. All the girls gasped.

"Why on earth would you want to go down there?" asked the redhead.

"We are guards transferred from Rochford. We are meant to guard the prisoners."

"Well then. What do you think, sissy? Who should take them?" asked the brunette.

"Let Barb. She isn't doing anything useful," said the redhead.

"And you are?" asked the blonde, who crossed her arms. "Go on then."

Barb, the blonde, stood from where she was sitting and stalked off. All of the boys followed. Gavin hurried ahead to meet with her and placed an arm around her waist. "A lovely girl as yourself shouldn't be upset about leading some guards around. I am not angry about their choice." The girl giggled.

After a long walk, the girl stopped in her steps. "Down the steps and then to your right." Barb stepped out of their way. Gavin stayed behind for a moment as Abraham and Phillius hurried down the steps. Abraham stopped and turned to look up at the doorway. Gavin laid a sharp kiss on the girl's lips. Abraham saw Phillius grinning, and then they both looked away.

"Let's go, boys," Phillius said, racing down the steps.

They heard shouts and cries as they walked through the dark halls. Gavin's nose kept moving around.

"Where would they usually put someone who's going to be beheaded?" Abraham asked, trying to keep up with Phillius.

"The tower. But for right now, let's just hope he's anywhere down here. The tower is harder to locate. Hey, puppy, stay with us, will you? We can't lose anyone down here."

Abraham and Phillius stopped and waited for Gavin. He was looking into each cell with amazement. All of a sudden, a hand shot out of one of the cells and took hold of Gavin's neck and pulled him in. He yelled in surprise. Instantly Phillius and

Abraham darted towards him. Abraham began pulling on Gavin while Phillius rose his hand to the prisoner. "Telos —"

"No, wait!" Gavin coughed. The hand let go of him and slowly pulled itself back into the cell as the figure moved forward. He was a tall, extremely dirty man with a long beard. Abraham looked at him closely, letting go of Gavin's waist. The man looked so familiar.

"Where did they take the girl?" Abraham asked aloud. Gavin looked over at him.

"I don't expect anyone down here would know," Gavin said. Abraham shook his head quickly.

"Sir, who are you?" Phillius asked towards the dark cell.

"The question is not who he is, but who I am, son."

Gavin tensed. Abraham pulled him over some. A tall man who was so skinny you could see his bones stepped out of the darkness and into view. Abraham squinted his nose.

"Solomon," Gavin said as if he were out of breath. The two stared at each other in silence. Phillius cleared his throat.

"Even though this seems like a very lovely get together, I think we should be going, don't you?" Phillius asked. Gavin was the first to run ahead, and each of the boys followed him.

"I will get out of here, Gavin! Just you wait! You'll regret stealing my life! You stole my life, mutt! What an honorable son you are! Ahhh!"

Abraham, Phillius, and Gavin hurried down the hallway until they reached a door and slammed it shut behind them. Gavin didn't say a thing. Abraham wanted to know what that was about, but he told himself not to ask. At least not now. But since when did Gavin have a psycho father?

They walked another fifteen minutes before coming to a stop. There was no sign of Derek. He was alive. He had to be.

CHAPTER 15

Cameron

"How could a girl like you create such power? Your people, as I hear, aren't meant to have what you do. Your people disgust me. Yet you do not. Why is this so?" Collin asked, pulling my hair to the side and placing his cheek on my shoulder. I was now dressed in a pale blue gown. I'd had to change in front of Collin, who hadn't seem to blink the whole time.

"Maybe you're twisted in your brain," I said, looking around the room. There had to be something I could use or a way to escape. *Come on, you guys.*

"The mouth on you appalls me, Anne. I am a bit insulted by your words, and it is a rare thing for me. We don't have to be enemies, you know. We could be more than friends...." Suddenly I was swung around and pushed back. I landed hard on the bench below his bed, and my head banged against the bedpost. Collin's eyes were slit. "We could be lovers, you and I. Do great things," he hissed and then kissed me. Actually, it was more like he was biting my face off so hard that he bit through my lip, and I began to bleed. I tried to pull from him, but his grip on my hands was super tight. I threw my head to the side, but it didn't faze him at all. He continued to kiss down my neck, and then he began to kiss my upper chest.

"Stop!" I yelled, and his hands moved quickly. One closed on both of my hands, cracking my wrists, and the other pressed down over my mouth. Collin pushed himself up off of me.

"Tsk, tsk, tsk. Naughty girl, you are," he said.

I watched him closely. He grabbed a pair of gloves off a nightstand next to his bed and then grabbed something next to it. I knew what it was automatically. He was so quick I didn't even see him when he reached me. He pulled my legs straight out and placed the chains around my ankles, and I yelled. He then placed another over my left wrist and then my neck. I didn't want to move. Instead, I glared up at him, heaving. Collin was smiling.

"I am so tired of being the victim!" I screamed, and my insides boiled. I was given these powers for a reason, and I needed to learn to use them! I lifted my free hand and threw it across his face. The pain when I moved was unbearable, but I knew I had to forget about the pain. I needed to do what I was meant to do, and that was to find Zalvana and make sure she was safe until they saved Derek. I didn't know why all of this had happened in my life, but I knew that I was gifted with all of this for a reason. Even if it did cost my life.

Collin's face stared at the ground for only a second before his hands pushed me back against the bedpost. I fought back. Sure, he was a man and also a Gathien, and this made him stronger. But I knew I could overpower him. I lifted my feet that were still chained together and pushed Collin off me. In that few seconds, I slid my small ankles out of the chains, blood running down them as they cut through them, and lifted my hands at Collin.

Please work…or something.

My light had to work. It had to!

Collin picked up the chains I had escaped from and lifted them at me. Come on…come on….

My whole body shook. "Come on!" I yelled. Collin thought of this as an invitation to fight, but I wasn't speaking to him. He was smiling as he swung the chain in the air. His nose was bleeding from my hit, and scratches went down his cheek. I pulled the gloves from my hands, and my palms exploded. The whole room glared from the light. It hurt, but it worked. Collin was thrown across the room and fell to the ground, unconscious.

"What was that?" one of the guards yelled, knocking on the door. "Sir?"

Think, think, think. Oh gosh!

Okay, this idea may be a stupid one, but I'd seen it in a movie once. Worth a try, I guess. I went over to the door where Collin was laying. He was knocked out cold. I pulled him to the side, letting his head bang against the floor before laying him down again and taking hold of his arm. I lifted my dress so that it showed all the way up to my upper thigh. I opened the door in a very small crack and then pulled Collin's hand up to my leg to rub it all the way up. The guards were quiet, and one cleared his throat. I put a smile on my face and quickly messed up my hair with my free hand before peeking out. I giggled, looking at the guards, who blushed. I wanted to laugh at myself. I bet it was a scene, and if Abraham was there, oh my goodness! "We'll need some privacy," I laughed. "Oh, stop it, Collin!" The guards just nodded and turned from me, still blushing. They looked super confused, though. When I shut the door, I dropped Collin's hand and hopped around in disgust. I quickly grabbed the gloves Phillius had given me and pulled them back on.

How was I going to get out of there? I looked about the

room.

The window.

Abraham

They searched all of the cells, but there was no sign of Derek. The boys leaned against the wall, thinking of what to do next. The only thing left to search was the tower, but Phillius kept saying it was too hard to get up there. But they had to at least try, didn't they? There was a lot of clinking and clanging outside, so Abraham looked out of the crack next to him. The guards were setting up for the execution and were nearly done.

"The only thing I can think of is the tower. But it would take more than me to get up there in time," Phillius said. "I could call a few of my friends, but again I don't think they would get here in time or even be willin' to help."

"Well, we can't let him die. I...what if you took your charm off Ca...Anne and find Derek instead?" Abraham asked.

"I would lose all contact with your sister if I did that."

"I understand that. But it's really important that we keep Derek safe. Gavin, I need you to do something for me. Phillius, can you...you know...poof out a piece of paper and a pencil for me?"

"Paper?" Phillius asked.

"A pencil?" Gavin asked, and the two looked at each other.

"Parchment and something to write with, then," Abraham said, scratching his forehead. Phillius shrugged, and then parchment and a feather appeared, with a floating container of ink next to them. Abraham caught them and sat them on the ground. He wrote a note quickly and then folded it. "Take this to Zalvana," he said.

"But we don't know where she is," Gavin said, taking the

note.

"Phillius said that wherever Cintia is, Zalvana will be there as well. You're a guard, Gavin, now start acting like one. Phillius, we need to get our plan going, and we need to be quick about it. Go, Gavin. I don't know what you are so afraid of in that tower but, come on, Phillius, lead the way."

Sawyer

Sawyer crossed his arms in annoyance. His lips were squeezed shut, and his throat was still tight. Jules stood in the same place with her hands still over her temples. Jack had sat back down, and his eyes were locked on his dead ex-wife.

"But no one knew of the charm except my family," Jules said, obviously speaking her thoughts out loud.

"We don't know exactly how Emily found out about the journal. It doesn't really matter now. She found it, and she used it. We say she's going to try and kill your ancestry, specifically Zalvana," Jack said calmly.

"But if she's killed…oh no. If she kills Zalvana, none of us will have existed! Cameron would have never gotten rid of that bastard." Everyone seemed to tense when she said, bastard. Her glow seemed so pure. At least they knew she wasn't some kind of angel. But she wasn't a demon either.

"If Emily succeeds, then everything will change. For me, you, and everyone who has been in contact with Cameron or our world. Gathiens will rule. What powers do you hold that a Gathien does also, Jules?" Jack asked.

"Strength and speed. The strength is usually given to the men and speed to the women. The light power is from our O'ahee line. I never expected Collin to be a pure being. I am just as lost as you. I see now, though, why it is time for Cameron to join us. She has been through so much. I never expected my potion to work."

"What was in that potion?" Jack asked once again. Everyone sat quietly and listened...other than Sawyer, who wasn't able to be loud at will. Otherwise, he would have spoken a long while ago.

"Old potions I read in our family books. It was to help our kind fight the Gathien part of ourselves. The painful part anyhow. I left that potion for you many years before just in case Cameron did become a Gathien. You had to have used it, didn't you, Jack? To help her ease the transition?" Jules burst out into tears...or a white liquid. She put her hands over her face then. "I have failed her! I knew Abraham cannot join us! From the very start when Abraham was born, I craved a daughter who could rightfully continue our line, and now it is ruined."

"Jules...," Jack said. It had to be the first time Sawyer had heard Jack speak so softly. "Why can't he join you? Why are they coming to Sawyer about Cameron?"

"Because!" she shrieked and threw her hands down. "The wolf has a strong hold on Cameron's heart! He has to let her go. She can't pick him over us! She can't!" She then placed her hands over her eyes again. "Abraham was touched by darkness. He joined Collin willingly. He is nothing to me."

Sawyer's heartbeat rose in anger. He stood from his chair and tightened his fists. His insides burned.

"Sawyer. Can you let him speak?" Jack asked Jules, who looked over at Sawyer for a long time before finally lifting a hand, and Sawyer could feel his throat release.

"Hold your tongue, Sawyer," Kimmeh said, and Sawyer gave her a nasty look.

"I know you love my daughter, and she loves you equally. Now, her heart is blocking us out. She's pushing what she is away. She doesn't realize if she pushes it away, it will expand and grow inside her until she cannot control it. She needs to be released," Jules said.

"You will not take her from me," Sawyer finally said, surprised by how his voice sounded fine.

"It is up to her, Jules. You can't force her to go with you," Jack said.

"You don't understand, Jack. This place is magical. You can be free. All of our ancestors live here—"

"Ancestors? Even Zalvana?" Sander asked.

"Yes."

"Can she talk to us too? Zalvana, I mean."

"No. I was given permission by our court. Zalvana has no such permission. She does not know about any of this, and I intend to keep it as such."

"Maybe she can help us!"

"How, when she is dead, just as I am?" The words she said were like ice.

"My memories are changin'. I think Cameron and Abraham are messing with me...with my past. How do we know they haven't messed up Zalvana's, too, if we don't ask her?" Gavin asked.

"I will ask her personally if anything has been odd. However, I will not tell her what is going on."

"How do we get Cameron back?" Sawyer asked.

"I do not know. What of you, warlock?" Jules asked, looking at Phillius, who looked up with a nervous grin.

"My idea? Well, I suppose a blood spell to this parchment."

"The same spell? You are the warlock who placed it upon the journal, am I correct?" she asked.

"The one and only. Though warlocks typically stay out of the business of anyone outside the warlock's law."

"Though you would place your bet into a war during the 16th century?" Sawyer asked.

"It was not a war then. Zalvana stopped it when she

married that Gaspard fellow. There is war now."

"No one is fighting," Sawyer said, lifting both of his thick eyebrows.

"Cameron. She is not in this realm. We must get her back," Jules said.

"You say 'Cameron this, Cameron that.' Does Abraham mean nothing to you?" Sawyer asked, taking a step closer to Jules, whose eyes slanted at his words.

"No. Abraham was a mistake from the moment he was born, and I blame Jack." Jack watched Jules speak, and at that moment, his face turned ill-looking, and he turned his gaze from Jules. "Abraham has a darkness inside of him he will never be able to release. Cameron is pure and a woman of our line. Such power should be kept safe... not used in a battle that will only lead to her death. Abraham made his bed, and he can sleep in it."

Sawyer shook his head at her explanation. His parents were always there for them until their terrible deaths, and not once did he ever feel unloved. It was at that moment he finally realized why Abraham was so private. Abraham knew, deeply, that his mother had never wanted him, and that angered Sawyer.

"He made his bed? The only reason you do not want him to join you is because he was born? You gave birth to him. You are the reason he is the way he is, not him. You should be the one sulking in your bed that you made. You will never get ahold of Cameron or her brother. I promise you that."

"Let's get this started then, shall we?" Phillius said, lifting himself from the couch. Jules tilted her head as if she were listening to someone whisper to her. She nodded to herself, and then she looked at Sawyer as if his words had meant nothing to her.

"You will bring her home?" she asked.

"Not if you're going to take her from me," Sawyer replied flatly.

Jules nodded her head again before turning from Sawyer and the group. "Take care of her, Jack," she said, and then she was gone. Everyone sat in silence until Gavin stood and exited the room without a word. Sawyer crossed his arms.

"Send me to her," Sawyer said, turning to the warlock.

CHAPTER 16

Cameron

"Freaking shit!" Movies made this look so freaking easy. "Freaking shit, ugh!" I yelled. I did my best not to look down. *Do not look down!* This was not a time to be scared of heights. The walls were deep, but I still felt as though I was going to pee myself. "Oh gosh," I whispered to myself.

I looked to my left to find an open window. The smell of food rose to my nose. I grabbed the wall, digging my nails into it while I took my other hand and reached for the opening. My hand grasped the edge, and I slowly pulled myself over until my foot was on the flat surface of the window sill. I peeked in.

A woman exited the room with a plate full of food. I was still a few stories high, and if I fell, I'd hurt myself badly, so I decided to chance entering the room. When my feet hit the floor, I ran to the door to look out. There was no one around, but someone could appear at any moment. I looked out again and then darted. The hallway wasn't long, but the question was what door I was supposed to take. When I reached the end of the hall, I pushed the door open slowly. Gladly it led to another hallway...at least I was getting somewhere. I then ran again, looking behind me every so often, and the last time I looked back to see if anyone was coming, I ran into something hard and fell forward on top of it.

I began to yell but caught myself. I looked down to see what I had run into, and a huge grin lifted my face. "Gavin!" I said and then hugged him. He didn't hug me back, though. I keep forgetting he wasn't my Gavin. It was weird because this Gavin was so different from my Gavin. I wondered why he had changed so much and how he had lived so long. "Where's my brother?" I asked while I sat up. Gavin slid from underneath me.

"They are goin' te tha tower. He sent me te take this te Zalvana," Gavin said, pushing his hair back, and then held out the paper to me.

I took it and then read. "'Stop the beheading. Cintia will be next if you don't.' Derek! Oh no! We have to…no! No, we have to get this to Zalvana. Come on!" Once we were both standing, I took hold of Gavin's collar and ran. I looked over at him. "What are you wearing?"

Gavin smiled.

We didn't speak during the entire run, and after a while, Gavin got in front of me and led the way. When we reached the same room I had seen before, I stopped and leaned up against the wall. "Do ye want me te take it in?" Gavin asked, out of breath. I looked up at the ceiling.

"No," I said. I knew I had to do this, but why was it so hard? "Just give me a minute," I said. Gavin looked around the corner and into the room and then looked over at me.

"I see her. She's sittin' on a bed with someone."

"A woman?"

"Yeah."

I pushed myself from the wall and peeked out like Gavin had done. Without looking at Gavin, I walked out and towards the room. I knocked on the open door softly. Cintia looked over at me, and her face went stern.

"Come in," I heard a voice say. I walked in. The room was huge, almost the size of Sawyer's whole downstairs. I looked at Cintia for a second before looking towards the fire, which was a bright blue. "Yes?" the voice called again. I looked to my left and could hardly believe my eyes. Her hair was a deep brown, and her eyes were hazel—as mine had been before I completed the change—except her eyes were wider. My hair wasn't as deep of a brown as hers, but it was close, and her hair was much longer. I felt like I was looking into a mirror, somehow. Until I realized it wasn't me I was seeing inside of her, but my mother.

"I...I have a letter for you," I said, placing the letter out towards her. She took it and read it silently. This had to be Zalvana.

"Who sent this?" she asked. "Who sent this letter?"

"A man. His name is Jack." Zalvana went still and then looked over at Cintia, who was looking at the piece of paper.

"Your name?"

"Her name is Anne Burgandy. But I've been questioning myself about that," Cintia said. Zalvana was looking at me now as Cintia walked over and stood between us. "This is the girl I was speaking of. The one Collin wants."

"Yeah, and we need to work fast, or else Derek is going to lose his head...literally," I said.

"I cannot. I must meet Gaspard in his chambers." Tonight was the night? Zalvana was going to get pregnant tonight? Oh no! Emily. I had to make sure Zalvana didn't get near Emily! But what about Derek? If he died, everything would change too. Anything that were to change would cause a ripple in our future, and I had to make sure that didn't happen.

Abraham

"We are going to get up there, and he's not going to be there," Abraham said, pulling his legs up the stairs.

"They haven't brought him down yet. If they had we—" There was suddenly a loud pounding of drums. Phillius stopped in his tracks and turned to look at Abraham with a blank face. "We would hear the drums." They both dashed down the steps, Abraham one step behind Phillius the whole time. The drums rolled and continued to do so. Abraham stopped for a moment to look out through some bars to see people surrounding the stage. He hurried down the steps.

"Can't you zap us out of here?" Abraham called.

"If I could, I would have zapped us to the top, ye moron! We have to get out of the tower before I can zap us out of here, as you call it! This place is concealed from magic."

Emily

"The drums!" she yelled, racing over to the dirt window. Her red hair fell down her front, with waves of it covering her bare skin. Her eyes sagged a little from lack of sleep, but she was wide awake now more than ever. She was so going to murder that little bitch today. Her plan had worked just as she hoped it would. There was a groan behind her and a rustle of covers being thrown. She turned to find her lover rubbing his beard-covered face.

"Meh god, girl, ye wake up te early."

"You've slept for days. I washed myself because you were so dirty I felt dirty myself," Emily replied, pushing her hair behind her and showing off her bare skin in the sunlight. He didn't seem fazed a bit by her attempt at catching his eye. This annoyed her.

"That mouth of ye's really is somethin', I tell ye. I do love it."

"Maybe I'll take you along then. Get dressed...we're

heading out," Emily said, crawling onto the bed and sitting on top of the man, who laid himself down. She let her hair fall over him as she looked down at him, tilting her head. Cameron was so dumb and would never figure anything out. Everything was turning out just the way Emily had planned, and the world Collin had sought to make for himself would come true, finally. "Well, if you behave, maybe I'll take you." The guard pulled her over so that he was on top of her. She grinned up at him, lifting her hands and stretching them around his neck. He closed in on her, and they kissed deeply until Emily bit his lip. He pulled back. "You know what I want, don't you? You know what I desire?" she asked, tracing his jaw.

"Yes," he said. Men were so naïve. "Ye wish me to aid ye. Ye wish me to kill Zalvana."

"Good. And what is next?" she asked.

"I kill the boy. I kill him, and I have ye," he said. Emily kissed him again.

"Yes, my lover, you will have me." She leaned up to kiss him again as she lied through her teeth but pulled back and rolled over off the bed. "Get dressed," she said, shutting the door behind her.

Cameron

The drums echoed down the hall. "What does that mean?" I asked, looking at Cintia, who looked really uneasy. She took a moment before answering me, and even then, I could still see the worry in her eyes.

"They are bringing Derek down for his —"

"No. We cannot let that happen, sister. Come." Zalvana hurried across the room and pushed over a bookshelf that led into a hidden back room. She pulled open a box in the wall and pulled out a bow and a holder full of arrows. Then she pulled out a knife, sword, and gloves that she handed to Cintia. "Cintia, you are skilled with a sword, so you take mine. Anne, do you know how to use a bow?" I looked at the bow, then back at Zalvana, who understood instantly and handed me a dagger instead that was connected to a very small black belt. I took it. "That goes around your thigh." They were acting like we were *Charlie's Angels* or something. I didn't do this. "The bow is simple. You hold it like this...." She raised it into the air, pointing it to the opposite side of me and Cintia, who was adjusting her own belt around her waist. "And place the arrow right here, you see? And then you pull it back like this. Understand?" she asked. I nodded. "If you can do this, Anne, you can use a bow. Here." I took it then and pulled it over my shoulder. "The gloves keep your hands from glowing," She smiled at me, handing me a pair of black gloves. I couldn't help but smile back. "If the warlock, Phillius, is helping you, then I do hope you don't need to use these. But if you must, I dare say do it without alarm." She knew Phillius?

Cintia placed her sword into her belt and pulled her hair into a tight braid. I pushed my hair, which had fallen out of its bun, behind my ears. Surely Phillius...no. I could. I thought only of my hair being pulled up into a tight bun and waited.

"What are you doing?" I opened my eyes, which I hadn't even noticed I'd closed, to find Cintia and Zalvana staring at me.

"My light won't work," I said.

"You're not from here. It would be odd if it worked perfectly fine, wouldn't it?" Cintia asked.

"Then why did that happen in the ball?"

"You are not from this time? I do not understand?" Zalvana asked.

"Too much to tell. But what happened to you is what the old stories call a 'blockage' holding in your light. Think of it as a vein that cannot flow blood, so soon enough, it clogs. You were holding it in, or perhaps it was because of the change in time for you. I am surprised it held in for even a few days' time. I would not be surprised if it happens again," Cintia said.

"What about my brother? Why hasn't he…you know?"

"I'm not sure about him. Your brother has a dark aura about him."

"A dark aura?"

The drums stopped. All of us went quiet. I even held my breath.

"Attention!" yelled a faint voice. Zalvana and Cintia moved again but quicker as they hurried from the small room and went over to the large open window. I followed and stood to the side of Zalvana, who stood in the middle, watching.

"Use your light, C." I looked over at Zalvana but found she was talking to Cintia and not me, "As much as possible. Be quick and be unseen. The death of Derek would be a sad one. You must be quick! I will distract Gaspard as much as possible. Go. Oh, Anne!" I had turned to follow Cintia out the door, but Zalvana called me back. I hurried back over to her. "Give this to your friend." It took me a moment to understand what she was talking about until I realized Gavin was still outside the door. Zalvana handed me a very small ring that would probably only fit Gavin's pinky finger. Gavin peeked his head in then as I looked out the door. He looked petrified. I held the ring out to him. He slowly took a few steps into the room and leaned in to take it from me. Gavin pulled it up close to his face and sniffed it. He was so weird these days. "Rosladine," Zalvana said, looking at Gavin, who finally looked up from the ring. "You've heard of it?"

"I thought they were myths."

"What's a Rosaline?" I asked, looking at the ring now. It

was silver and had writing on it that I couldn't read.

"Ros-la-dine. It increases the powers of a higher being. A Were like him. It would not work for either of us, of course, but to a Gathien, it is very powerful. It belonged to Gaspard's eldest son, James, who died a few years ago. I advise you not to wear it for a long period of time." It was a warning, I could tell.

"It killed him, didn't it? The power was too much for him, just like my clog was to me," I said.

"Partly," she replied without looking at me. "He died during his transformation. The ring was supposed to cause him to become a powerful Gathien before he even was one, but instead, he became so willing to it, it killed him."

"So all Gathiens go through the change? That means all Gathiens were once human."

"Exactly. They can be stopped, Anne."

Gavin placed the ring on his pinky finger just as I had expected. It explained why the ring was so small, though. Gathiens were usually very thin but extremely strong. Weres were well built…well, except the girls. Girls were just twice as strong. The drums started again.

"We have to go! Come on!" Cintia said from the door and ran into the hallway, Gavin following her. I turned quickly towards Zalvana and went to her. I threw my arms around her and hugged her tightly.

"Thank you!" I said before racing after Cintia and Gavin. *Thank you not only for being so brave but for showing me that we are capable of doing anything.* "Hey! You guys!" I said, barely seeing Gavin go around the corner. "Wait up!" I said, quickening my pace. "Gav —" I turned the corner, and my heart stopped.

"Hello, Zalvana." Emily stood there with her arms held out beside her. Why did she call me Zalvana? "I've been waiting for you."

CHAPTER 17

Abraham

"The door! Hurry!" Phillius yelled, pointing to the door.

Abraham made his feet move faster as Phillius raced ahead of him. The moment they pushed through the door, Phillius took hold of Abraham's shoulder, and there was a loud pop. Everything went black, and Abraham couldn't see anything. It was nothing like his light travel. The light travel was bright, and he could see around him in blurs, but with Phillius, there was nothing but black. His feet suddenly made contact with the hard flooring, and slowly everything came into view. He wanted to throw up.

"It's much faster than an O'ahees transport. The sickness will fade," Phillip said, clapping Abraham on the back, who held his forehead and heaved.

"Jack!" Abraham turned around to find Cintia and Gavin running up to them. "We jus' passed tha northern windows, and tha are leadin' Derek out!" Gavin said. Abraham looked at them over and over, trying to figure something out. He glanced up at Gavin and then to Cintia. He looked at Cintia's eyes, that had turned tired and a pale green. His eyes widened, looking behind them.

"Where's Ca...Anne?" he asked. Gavin looked back too.

"She was right behind us."

"You go ahead...I will go look for her," Cintia said, handing Abraham her sword.

"You may need this—" Abraham started, but Cintia cut him off.

"No. I will be fine. You'll need it more than I. Now go!" When Cintia was out of sight, Gavin, Abraham, and Phillius ran in the opposite direction towards the opening hall.

"So what's tha plan now?" Gavin asked, running behind the two. "Obviously, our first plan didn' work!"

"I suppose we will just wing it, right, Jack?" Phillius said, winking at Abraham as they ran. "Whoa!" Skidding to a stop, Phillius nearly fell forward, with Gavin and Abraham running into him. "Guards," he whispered, pushing the boys behind him. Abraham looked around him.

"We are guards, remember?" Abraham said, looking over at Phillius, and then they all looked down at themselves. After sharing glances, they each entered the hall. Abraham straightened his back and placed both of his arms at his side in a soldier stance.

"Bloody light lover. How long did he expect us to not know?" one of the guards said.

"I say that lover of his should be executed too. We all know she is just like the rest of them. Hoarding light people in her home."

"The light girl has not been found, and I'm sure once they do, she will be executed with the rest of them."

"The other light girl turned herself in this morning. They say Collin had his way with her before they...." He gestured his finger across his throat, making a disturbing noise as he did it. Abraham's insides boiled.

"Why not execute her with her lover? Why do it in secret?"

"It was more fun, I suppose. You know Collin."

Abraham tensed up in anger. Apparently, Phillius could see it as he elbowed him in the side. The guards looked over at them as they passed. "Oi, what're you lookin' at?" asked one of the guards. Phillius took hold of Abraham's arm and pulled him along.

"You don't think tha' captured yo' sista while we ran, do ye?" Gavin asked.

"Let's hope not." Why would they capture Cameron and not Gavin or Cintia as well? It didn't make any sense. He knew they were after Cameron, but since Gavin and Cintia helped her escape, wouldn't they have captured them as well because they had helped her? Not unless Cameron wasn't captured by the guards. Then who...? No...she couldn't know....

"This is a distraction," Abraham said out loud. "I have to find Anne."

"No. We have to save Derek. Remember? Cintia will find her. Look...."

When they got to the side entrance that led out to the courtyard, they found themselves surrounded by townspeople, who were shouting and causing chaos. Abraham's eyes searched the grounds until he found Derek. The drums could barely be heard. Derek was standing beside two guards with his hands tied behind him, and his eyes were wide, looking at the pedestal where he would lay his head. "If anything, we need to be the ones causing the distraction," Phillius continued.

"What do'ye think about him?" Gavin asked. Abraham looked back at him and then past him. The executioner was walking towards them to go to the courtyard. Gavin gave his usual grin. Abraham knew instantly what he was thinking. But he couldn't seem to keep the thought of Cameron from his mind.

Sawyer

"I don't understand why it will not work," the warlock said as he examined the piece of parchment.

"Or you are being stopped from doing it. You heard Jules. She said for me to stop you. They won't let you go to the past," Jack said.

"They know the law," Kim said quietly. "The law states no time travel, and not only that, she hates Sawyer."

"When has anyone ever messed with time travel?" Kyle asked.

"No one that I've heard of. I guess it's because warlocks have that power. But you were so sure," Kimmeh said, looking at the warlock.

"I do not go by your laws. Warlocks have not for years. Being Were's, I suppose you cannot travel," Phillius said.

"There has to be a way to do it," Sawyer said, placing his hands on his head. "You can't do anything? Nothing at all?"

"No. I suppose I could travel on my own to find your light people, but you cannot. I'm sorry."

"Then go!"

"I will not go."

"But...you can't leave them."

"Are they smart?"

"What?" Sawyer asked, wild at his question. It nearly made his head explode.

"Are they smart? These siblings?"

"Yes, they are," Jack said.

"Then they will find a way."

"But they're facing Emily," Kimmeh said.

"Who is merely a Gathien. Just like her brother," Phillius replied.

"You are leaving them to die," Sawyer said slowly, letting his hands fall down and looking to the grass that was now underneath his feet.

Phillius looked at him. "If you do not believe they can survive, then I suppose you will need to buy a couple of headstones to add to your collection."

Sawyer growled.

Cameron

I just couldn't believe it. How could Emily not know that I was not Zalvana? We looked a lot alike, but we weren't exactly twins! Emily really was Collin's sister...both complete idiots. "Gaspard will know about your plans," Emily said. I didn't answer her. "He will destroy *every*thing like you. Gathiens will rule!" I stared at her without making a sound. My hair was falling down again, but Emily didn't seem to notice. "Henry, dear. Can you come here, please?" I looked to my left to see a man with a beard covering his face, who was dressed as a guard. "I do believe we had an agreement about a certain boy...."

"Yes," the man replied. No, he didn't just say it. He spat it out.

"You can go now. Kill him however you please. I'll take care of her." Emily cocked her head towards me as the man left the room. Kill who? I was so confused. I couldn't yell for help because she would immediately know who I was. Then again, I couldn't use my powers because they were going crazy. *Come on, guys, get to Derek...stay together.* "Now back to you. Do you want to die fast, or would you rather die a slow, painful death?" I locked my jaw. "Speak!" Emily screamed, throwing her hands forward and scratching my face. I cried out as the skin ripped from my face. She did this multiple times, like a cat with a scratching board. She seemed to have totally lost it...she even growled at me. "All because of you!" she yelled, pushing herself from me. "My brother...my family...my people are all gone because of you! Filthy light that you all carry!"

Then it hit me. If she killed me, she would think she'd killed Zalvana. If she killed me, then my friends and family would be safe. Abraham could take care of her. I knew it.

"You are a very stupid girl. Very stupid." She rose from me and stepped back. One hand rose to her forehead while the other was placed on her waist.

Abraham

"It's a little big." Gavin stepped out of the hallway with his face covered with a black mask. "And I'm a werewolf. It's hard for us to not fit in things." Abraham couldn't help but let out a low laugh, looking at the clothes that were practically hanging off Gavin.

"Here, hold still." Phillius walked around Gavin, looking him up and down with a strange look. He lifted his pointer finger, and there was a flash of blue light. The clothes on Gavin began to shrink.

"Brilliant!" Gavin said, looking down at himself. Abraham turned to look out the window.

"Where's Gaspard and Collin?" Abraham asked, letting his eyes switch to Phillius and Gavin, who both looked at him in return.

"Gaspard never goes to a beheading. He's probably with Zalvana right now. Collin? Who knows. He does what he wants," Phillius replied.

"Bastard," Gavin whispered in his strong Scottish accent.

"You may say a few words!" yelled someone.

Abraham, Phillius, and Gavin peeked through the window. Abraham felt helpless without his powers. Derek's eyes closed for only a moment before reopening. This time they weren't wide, but their normal size. His body had seemed to loosen as he took a few steps forward to look down at the crowd.

"Go, Gavin. I'll give you the signal," Phillius said, pushing Gavin towards the door. After a slight hesitation, he went out towards the crowd. People moved from his path as he went towards the stage. Derek caught sight of him, and his face went very pale. Still, he straightened his back and lifted his chin. Gavin, looking like the executioner, climbed onto the stage.

"I am innocent." Derek paused as Gavin took his place next to him and then continued. "O'ahee people are blessed by God. If you don't support them, you're not going for God, whom has rested his power upon them to keep us safe. I love an O'ahee woman and am proud to call her my own. To you, it is discrimination against our human race, but to me, it is right. She is my sunlight. She is your daylight, and I will stand here to proclaim my love for Cintia Peythron willingly. Hate me so. Take my head and lay it on your pedestal! But I will be greeted by death as a friend." Derek glanced at the crowd before taking a step back.

"Come," Phillius finally said. Abraham did so.

CHAPTER 18

Abraham

Abraham walked to the side of the stage, the side where Derek would lay his head. Gavin stood on the other side with an axe in his hand while Phillius mixed himself into the crowd. Derek was looking at Gavin, not knowing who he truly was. Everyone was quiet in the crowd — clouds formed in the sky, covering the sunlight. Abraham's palms burned, and he squeezed them shut. *Not now*, he thought, *not like Cameron… please.* He placed his arms behind his back and straightened himself. The drums started again, but they were much slower.

Abraham looked up to the stage again to see Derek's arms were untied, and he fell to his knees, looking up at the sky. There was soft thunder, but no rain came. Gavin moved to Derek's side as Derek laid his head forward against the block. *Come on, Phillius*, he thought again. *Come on!* Gavin raised the axe into the air. However, Gavin's eyes looked at Abraham, who tightened his jaw, looking from him and to the crowd. He searched for Phillius.

"May God have mercy on your soul!" said the speaker.

Abraham's eyes snapped to look up at Derek and Gavin. Gavin's arms were frozen in the air. He then closed his eyes for a moment before they flew open. He strengthened his grip on the axe and then threw his arms forward and then down. Abraham went forward without any thought.

Cintia

She had never felt so brave in her life. Always the youngest, always the less brave. Zalvana had always been on top since she and Cintia were the only ones who had survived to their adult years. Her father had even favored Zalvana over her. She raced down the hall, dodging any guards that came into view. "Anne?" she called when she entered an empty hall. Her eyes traveled the halls looking for any evidence of Anne. Then she found an arrow pushed into a crack of the wall... Anne's arrows that she was given by Zalvana. Collin had captured her. She knew it. But she didn't want to believe it.

She placed the arrow in her belt, then walked down the nearest pathway. She glanced in an open room to find nothing there but a table and a few chairs. Then a faint scream echoed into Cintia's ears, and she ran towards it, following the echo. Her palms warmed, and then her body felt light as the light surrounded her. Still, her feet moved over the cold floor. Cintia found herself outside a room, one that she had never visited before, and the door was closed. Cintia went to open it but stopped herself and instead placed her ear against it. Another scream was heard...a scream of anger. She went for her sword, but it wasn't there. She cursed at herself for giving it to Jack. She placed a hand against the door then, and it cracked.

Cameron

I didn't understand why she hadn't killed me yet. Her screams of fury made me jump every time. She threw things across the room, and she mumbled things I couldn't hear.

I had never considered, until now, the possibility that she wasn't just pissed off...she was grieving. The loss of Richard hurt enough, and I knew if I ever lost Abraham, I would go on a rampage. She'd lost her brother. I hadn't even realized how much she did lose. Everyone in her coven were only part Gathien, created by Collin with one of his powers, and the Gathien part of them died when Collin died. Except her. I felt sorry for her. But then again, I was scared and angry too.

Emily was turned away from me. I tried my best to be quiet as I tried to squeeze my hands from the rope. Behind me, I heard a soft click. I looked at Emily, but she didn't seem to have noticed. I quickly turned back to see the door coming open slowly. I kept switching from Emily to the door, my heart racing, and when Cintia came into view, I felt myself loosen and quietly let out a breath of relief.

Cintia looked at me for a second, wild-eyed, before moving to me in a swift crawl. She pulled a very small knife from her breast (I had no idea how she'd put it in there without hurting herself) and went down to cut through my rope hold. Suddenly she was lifted and then thrown. I gasped, watching her until she landed on the ground with a loud thud. I looked up to find the male guard, who stood over me. Emily turned around in a quick motion.

"We have a visitor," the guard said.

"I thought I told you to kill the boy while you had the chance! I have this under control. Men!" Emily hissed. "They never do anything right!"

"I do believe if I hadn't seen this girl here coming, you would have been dead." To my disbelief, Emily just waved his comment aside. He turned from her and picked Cintia up, dragging her over to me. She laid limp on the ground. I heard another drumbeat, but it was only a few pounds. They were slow too. Emily went to the window, and then a large grin appeared on her face. She turned to me.

"See what your people have caused?" I tried to ignore her, but it was just so hard. My ears listened to the outside. My heart raced again. "Such a pity," she said then and turned from me once again, but this time she went over to a table near the front of the room. I jumped when something touched my thigh. I looked over to find Cintia. She pulled my gown up and then took my dagger from my thigh pouch. Her eyes were still shut. There was a little light, and the dagger lifted on its own. I looked over at Henry, who was staring at the doorway. The dagger cut through my rope. Henry turned to us, and I quickly took hold of the dagger and pushed it underneath my gown. His boots clicked while he walked.

"May God have mercy on your soul!" yelled a faint voice.

There was silence again until a bunch of gasps and screams were heard. I closed my eyes and held in my tears. They couldn't have killed him! They couldn't have! Not Derek! Not because of me! Abraham had to save him…if not, we wouldn't exist anymore. We would have changed something in history that hadn't happened before. I wanted to burst out and cry so bad. Why did I cause so much trouble? Why did I cause people to die? I never wanted that to happen! I would disappear into nothingness.

Abraham

Abraham's hands landed on the stage. Only a mere second longer and Derek would be gone. His whole life would be over, all because of Abraham's selfishness! Suddenly there was a shatter, and Abraham looked up to find the axe split into pieces only inches from Derek's neck. The pieces glided around like the planets did around the sun. Many people gasped, and a few screamed at the sight.

Phillius came through the gawking crowd, his eyes staring

at the handle that was once an axe. Abraham looked at Derek, who looked up at the floating pieces. His mouth was half-open. Gavin lifted his mask to look at Abraham, waiting for the next move. Abraham shrugged. The pieces fell, crashing against the stage. Phillius then threw his hand up, and the pieces transformed into snakes. They slithered towards the crowd, which scattered with yells and screams.

"Let's go!" Abraham yelled.

Derek seemed to snap out of then because he stood. He paused to look at Gavin before hopping off the stage with Gavin following. They each ran towards the woods, which was their meeting destination since it was the easiest place to reach. Cintia, however, wouldn't know the spot unless she found Cameron. Cameron had to be fine. She always was. "Now, what do we do?" Gavin asked, taking a canteen from Phillius, who'd grabbed it from the back of their wagon.

"We wait," Abraham said.

"How will we know if they need us?"

"We'll know." Abraham sat against a tree, looking towards Collin's home quietly. The others chatted amongst themselves while Gavin was attempting to make a fire using wood and also while Phillius laughed at him by flickering fire in his fingertips.

Sawyer

He hurried back into his home, leaving Phillius by himself as he chanted silently and straight to a room down the hall. The door was shut. "Gavin! You stay in my home by invitation, and I command you to open this door! Now!" Sawyer yelled, banging on the door. There was silence until the door lock clicked and the door came open. Sawyer entered the room that had once belonged to Kimmeh and Danny to find Gavin walking towards the window. "They will not allow me to travel. You say you have thoughts of Cameron you never have before, and you *will* tell me what's going on! What are you keeping from us?" Gavin kept his back to Sawyer without a word. "Answer me!" Sawyer roared. Gavin turned around, his shoulders pulled back. He yelled too, storming at Sawyer, who didn't flinch. Two wolves fighting for their rightful place as pack leader.

"Guys!" Sawyer and Gavin continued to stare each other down. There was a sound of feet, and then Rebecca stood there.

"Sawyer, our packs are allies; why do you think we would betray you?" Gavin asked.

"He's a protector; they are limited on what they can say! Gavin...he's...he's not my brother. He's my uncle. My great uncle!" Rebecca threw herself between them.

"What are you saying?" Sawyer asked, pulling himself away from Gavin and staring at him in wonder and shock.

"I was around when...when, uh...," Gavin began, but his throat seemed to tighten every time he tried to speak. Rebecca placed a hand on his arm.

"When Zalvana was alive," she said. Gavin nodded.

"I was the same age as Rebecca when she....." He seemed to be having trouble speaking.

"It's okay, Gavin. When Zalvana was alive, so was Gavin. Of course, I don't know all of it. When Zalvana had a child with a Gathien, Gavin would have only been a teenager. My great grandfather was Gavin's brother. He wasn't a good man, so Gavin helped my family through all of these generations. He's my uncle. He's not my brother."

"What does this have to do with Cameron?" Sawyer asked.

CHAPTER 19

Cameron

My stomach wasn't agreeing with me. I felt as if I hadn't eaten in days, and I was quite ready for someone to put me out of my misery already. My head was pounding through my skull. It wasn't like me to give up.... though with everything I had suffered in only a few days' time was finally placing a toll on my mind and body.

Shut up, Cameron. Enough complaining.

"You can take her. I'll take care of Miss Peythron." The guard took hold of Cintia and began to drag her from the room. I shrieked and grabbed for her. My hands were free, and I had totally forgotten till now. I flung myself forward and threw my arms around her. She looked up at me and raised her hand. The dagger laid on the ground where I'd left it, but it flew to us, and I caught it, jabbing it into the guard's leg. He yelled in agony.

"Go!" I yelled. Cintia quickly grabbed her bow and arrows that were placed next to the door, and then she raced to the door. Before I joined her, I yanked the dagger from the guard's leg and rushed to Cintia's side. Emily stopped us at the door with her fingernails deep in the walls.

"Move," Cintia said, raising the bow that had an arrow placed in it. Emily looked down at the guard, who was holding his leg, then she looked at us. I could see the veins in her forehead pulsing.

"I have gone through too much to have you let her escape!" Emily launched at us. Cintia pushed me aside, letting go of the arrow. My eyes followed the arrow as the sharp point flew through the air and into Emily's chest, on the opposite side from her heart.

"The window!" Cintia yelled, pulling me with her. She wasn't slowing down as we ran towards the window, which was barely even cracked open. We were going to go through it, and I knew I had to brace myself. Emily yelled out in pain, causing the room to shake. "Trust me!" Cintia said, taking my hand into hers. I was ready for it. I closed my eyes and heard the glass break. Hands clawed into my back. The air made my hair fall from its pin, and it flew up as we fell. It all happened so fast. I looked up to see red hair blocking my view. Emily grabbed for me with something in hand, and there was another scream — my scream — and then came the pain. I saw light and heard a faint yell of "Anne!"

Abraham

"Look!" Abraham yelled, standing up from the ground. A bright light exploded out of the large estate. It fell like a falling star and then disappeared into nothing. Derek came up to his side, letting out a sigh of relief.

"Cintia," Derek said before looking over at Abraham, who had glanced over at him when he spoke. "That was her light. They are safe."

"How do you know?"

"Her light has always been the brightest I've ever seen. Her heart may be stubborn," he laughed a little as he rubbed his beard, "but she cares for so many. I love her for that, you know. It's wrong to love one of your servants, let alone an O'ahee creature. But I do. Very much so. Cintia wouldn't let anything happen to your sister, I assure you."

"Where do you think she took them then? They aren't here."

"They might have needed to join the others where their powers are heightened. My guess? Glowering Falls. It's a secret fall that only certain people can find. Magical beings. Mostly O'ahee creatures. If they were hurt even the slightest, that's where Cintia would go. I know it."

"But you've been there?"

"I have, with Cintia's permission."

"What do we have to do?"

"Do what you O'ahee people do, I suppose. Your people will hear you." Abraham looked back at Phillius and Gavin, who were talking beside the fire. The sun was just going down. He looked back at Derek before shutting his eyes. "Let everything disappear from your mind. Think only of where your destination lies." The crackle of the fire was the last thing he heard.

Bright light formed behind his closed eyes. He opened them to find an incredible landscape with lights glittering out of the waterfall. He looked up at the sky that was lit with a bright blue hue. It was like Heaven. The grass beneath his feet seemed untouched and was the brightest green he had ever seen. Lands expanded as far as the eye could see. Even the air was inviting and pure. He wondered if this place still existed in his time. Would he be able to return to it? He could hope. A place of his people that he would have never known had it not been for Emily. Though he would not thank her for it. If it hadn't been for the scream, he would have forgotten about everything that had happened.

He ran as fast as he could, following the yells as his eyes adjusted to the light quickly. Once coming to the other side of the waterfall, he found long red hair crazily flying around and another form struggling beneath it. "Jack!" Cintia was leaning against the edges of the water before him. Her body looked so fragile and broken. He went towards her, but she raised her hand in protest. "No, it's your sister! Go to her!" She stopped him from helping her and pointed to the fiery red hair. Emily. The girls were fighting each other with agonizing blows.

"Cameron!" he yelled. The two girls stopped for only a mere second. Emily looked back at Abraham. Her face was scratched, and blood ran down her face and dripped into her hair. Cameron rose up and pulled Emily down onto the ground before hitting her, and then rose to her feet. She clumsily stepped back. Blood soaked Cameron's stomach. Abraham wasn't sure if it was hers or Emily's, but he didn't wait to find out. He tried to go to her but was blocked by an unknown force.

They do not wish for you to interfere. Cintia's voice echoed in his mind. He looked back to her to find that she was now standing and looking at him.

Emily rose to her feet, facing Cameron.

Who was "they"? *Who?* Abraham asked.

Our people want to see if Cameron is worth saving.

Abraham looked at her in awe. He had never told her their true identities. Cintia only smiled at him. The situation seemed to disappear from her mind as she seemed calmer than he. "You know? You've known all along?" he asked her, taking a step forward.

"Of course I knew." She looked up to the sky. "Our people once told me I would be visited by those who would need my help and guidance. Both of my blood, both of my family, and both that hold great value in our future. You both are special because you have proved the impossible. Both Gathien and O'ahee. You and your sister have to decide, eventually, who will continue with this prophecy and who should continue with our people. Everything happens for a reason, Abraham Evans, and you need to believe. Allow Cameron to decide her fate on her own." There was a flash of light, and Cintia was gone. Something small landed on his feet, and right away, he knew what it was.

Zalvana's journal.

Cameron

The pain was agonizing. My stomach was beating against the hole where the blood flooded from me. I looked to Emily, whose arm hung limply, and I knew she couldn't use it. "I didn't do this to ruin your life!" I yelled, holding my stomach. Emily glared at me, pushing her hair from her face.

"You don't know me," she hissed.

"I do. It's me. I'm Cameron."

Emily's face fell from anger to shock. She shook her head. "You…you…no!" she shrieked.

"Collin was evil! It doesn't mean you have to be the same!"

"I will avenge him. I will do what he couldn't, and that is to kill your entire line!" She raced at me, but I stood my ground.

"Cameron!" I looked over at Abraham, who stood a few feet away from me, waving his arms. Emily pushed me to the ground, attacking me. The pain was horrible, and I used all my strength to push her off my body. I lay my head on the ground and looked to my left and saw a small black object that shined in the light. Zalvana's dagger…the same dagger I'd used on the guard and the same dagger that Emily had placed in my stomach. I clenched my hands into fists and pounded

Emily until she fell to the side, and then I kicked her away
from me. I forced myself to crawl for the dagger. My foot was
grabbed and tugged back, but I pulled it from Emily's grasp
and kicked her again, this time on the face. Quickly I went for
the dagger.

Cameron! Abraham's call!

Ab? Ab, I can hear you!

*It's this place…it's O'ahee land. I can't come to you. You need
to destroy her! I know what to do!*

I'm trying! But it hurts!

What hurts?

My stomach…the dagger….

"An arm versus a stomach. I'd go for the arm," Emily said
in a taunting tone. Blood was pouring from her nose. She was
able to stand and grab the dagger before me, and in defeat, I
turned onto my back and lay there, coughing and heaving.
My eyes were dry, and my body felt hollow.

Cameron, get up!

My eyes went over to Abraham, but I didn't move the rest
of my body. My lips were parched, and it was beginning to be
hard to breathe. My body was flat against the grass. I let my
fingers slide through the grass that felt soft and cool. Emily
stood over me, dagger in hand.

Cameron!

With an evil laugh, Emily placed both of her hands
around the dagger. "I would ask if you had any last words.
But I could care less." She raised her arms up, and I could see
the pain in her eyes from forcing her arm up.

No!

I closed my eyes. My heart was slowing, and all of a
sudden, I couldn't even feel the pain. The grass turned from
cool to warm. Suddenly I felt pressure on my chest, and
the ground turned hot underneath me. I could have sworn

I opened my eyes, but all I saw was black. The land wasn't there anymore, and I wasn't there anymore. I heard a loud swoosh sound and yelling, but I couldn't understand any of the words. Hands were placed on my arm, and suddenly my body felt light. But still, I could see nothing.

"Cameron, stay with me!" Abraham's voice again. I could feel him next to me. "We're back! We're home! Sawyer's coming! Stay with me!" I was then staring at a bunch of blurred colors, but at least I could see.

Sawyer

"So you really had nothing to do with this?" Sawyer asked, now sitting on a chair near the window. He looked at Gavin for the longest time before looking to the floor. All this time, he'd had such hatred for Gavin. From the beginning, Gavin had a strong relationship with Cameron that Sawyer never understood until now and had held her heart for some reason. It wasn't that Cameron loved Gavin, it was that she trusted him, and he had helped her when Sawyer was unable to. All those months Sawyer had been captured by Collin, Gavin was the one that watched over Cameron and took care of her. It was Gavin's job, in a way, to help special people like Cameron, and Sawyer couldn't hate Gavin for that. He should thank him.

"I became a protector after I saved a man's life. A...a creature of O'ahee came to me. A woman. She told me to do something, and instantly I became a protector. All these years, my memory was limited because my protector abilities are only growing by the day. It was a gift that was supposed to be my father's, and ever since, he's hated me for it. I will live until the rest of you are gone and after. I was selfish—"

"No, I was selfish for thinking otherwise. I'm sorry for the way I have treated you and your pack. I understand you can't tell us everything, and I don't expect you to. But I would appreciate it if you both," he looked to Gavin and then to Rebecca, "Would join me back downstairs so we can speak to Phillius."

Sawyer let out a long exhale. Gavin smiled at him then, and Sawyer smiled back, nodding his head to him. Rebecca ran ahead and down the steps, leaving Gavin to follow, then Sawyer. Upon arriving downstairs, everyone was still waiting in the living room except Phillius until he came in behind them.

"I remember them now!" Sawyer, confused, looked to Phillius, who now stood next to the large fireplace that was lit with blue flames. The warlock's eyes were large and aware as Gavin and Sawyer both went to his side.

"I remember her." Phillius held a picture in his hand. Sawyer glanced down at it to find it was a photo of himself and Cameron from her birthday party a month ago when she'd turned twenty. He glanced back up at Phillius, who returned the gaze. "Anne…," he said, almost in amazement. "Anne and her brother. Do you remember, Gavin? We helped Cintia. I was much younger, and so were you!"

Gavin shook his head and laughed. "It *was* Cameron!"

Suddenly a bright light filled the room from the outside, and everyone gasped. Phillius scurried over to the front window and flung open the curtains. Gavin and Sawyer rushed over to the window, too, to find Abraham kneeling at a figure's side. Sawyer's heart sank, but his feet moved. He hurried from the home and ran to Abraham but flung himself down on the other side of Cameron's body. She breathed heavily, and there was a gurgling sound coming from her throat. He burst into tears, looking down at her as she looked out to nothing. Trying to keep her from bleeding out, he placed his hands onto her stomach.

"Cameron...," he whispered to himself as a sense of pain curled through his body. "Cameron!" Sawyer yelled. She looked up at the stars but didn't seem to see him at all. He looked to his right to find the dead body of Emily, which lay only a few feet away. Her eyes were wide open and lifeless. Sawyer looked down at Cameron again. "Oh, Cameron, look at me!" Sawyer said. When he saw the blood covering her torso, his hand went to it and pressed onto it as if to stop the blood from flowing out. "Cameron, my love, look at me," he whispered, placing his forehead to hers. Abraham fell back onto his bottom in front of him and lifted his hands onto his own head. His breathing was unsteady, and he shook frantically.

"It...it...she.... At the last second, it let me pass. I took the knife, and I...I...I killed Emily!" Abraham yelled.

"Calm yourself, Abraham, come on." It was Jack that came to Abraham's aid, pulling his son into his arms and holding him as tears burst from his eyes and moans of sadness escaped his lips. Sawyer only looked to them for a second before returning his eyes to Cameron's.

"You're a smart man! Save her!" Sawyer yelled without looking at Jack again. He'd saved her once. He could save her again. "Save her, please!" he pleaded, still holding her wound.

"I can't help her —" Jack began.

"No! Dammit! Now save her! Now! Save her!" Sawyer cried out, pulling Cameron into his arms.

CHAPTER 20

Cameron

I couldn't speak or move, but I could hear and feel. Sawyer pulled me into his arms. Tears filled my dry eyes, and I tried to speak, but nothing came out, nor did I think I even moved. "Cameron, I love you," Sawyer said to me so softly. It was like he was talking to a sleeping baby. It was also the first time he had ever told me he truly loved me. "Do you hear me? I love you." I heard Abraham to the other side of me, and I wanted to tell him it was okay. I wanted to tell all of them it was okay and that this was what was meant to be. I had done what I needed to do. There was another scream and then a hard thud next to me from Sawyer's side.

"Do something!" It was Kimmeh.

"Cameron, no!" I heard Danny cry and heard him fall next to Kimmeh.

"Move!" Then it was Sander's voice. I saw a blur move away, and then two figures come into view. I felt hands being placed on me and then a sharp spray of warmth. But still, I could not breathe. Still, I felt the blood spill.

"I can't...we can't. It's not working." Abigail. Sander and Abigail were trying to heal me.

"There's nothing I can do," Jack said faintly. I could feel my body going light. I was going to die, and I wasn't so sure I wanted to. Hearing Sawyer's voice made me open my eyes, figuratively speaking, and I still had so much to do. I knew I had done what I was meant to, and I finally knew who I truly was—an O'ahee creature. My thoughts were interrupted at the sound of Sander's voice once more.

"The wound is...it's changing color. As if the object that was—"

"A knife! A knife was stabbed into...into her stomach!" I heard Abraham say.

"The knife was poisoned by something. I can't cure poison," Jack said, almost breathless.

There was a bright light ahead of me, and I saw a figure.

Let go, darling.

Mom?

You need to let go.

But Sawyer.... But everyone —

They will understand. Join me. Come to your people.

Mom, I didn't mean for any of this to happen.

Because of you, everyone is safe. Your time is over. You did what you were meant to do. Come.

I saw her then. She looked the exact same as I remembered, except for the golden robe she wore.

"I need you," I heard a voice say. Then I heard a musical song. A loud whistle and it instantly reminded me of Eden. "Stay with me, please, Cameron," I heard Sawyer say before I closed my eyes, trying to pull from the darkness that was trying to take me. I loved him so deeply, but my body felt as if I hadn't slept in months. I was weak. My body was tingly, and I heard my heartbeat in my ears. But then I couldn't feel... couldn't feel it.... I....

"Cameron!"

Next Book in the Series:
Darkened Shadows: The Discovery

Now Available
Darkened Shadows: The Call

Before You Go...

HELP AN AUTHOR

write a review

THANK YOU!

Share your voice and help guide other readers to these wonderful books. Even if it's only a line or two, your reviews help readers discover the author's books so they can continue creating stories that you'll love. Log in to your favorite retailer and leave a review. Thank you.

About the Author

Amber Watkins began writing the Darkened Shadows series in her teens and has enjoyed writing her whole life. Darkened Shadows is very close to her heart and a story she will forever cherish. She also loves playing with her pets, reading, and being in the great outdoors.

www.ingramcontent.com/pod-product-compliance
Lightning Source LLC
Chambersburg PA
CBHW030331180626
46810CB00003B/1307